Caleb and Mary Ruth are now older and closer to the Lord. It is now the years of the 1970's and early 80's. They are teaching people and following their true destiny. Other things are happening and it is making them stronger and stronger and helping others to believe in our Lord and Savior, Jesus Christ. They now have a group of wonderful Christians helping them. Also getting stronger to teach and help others. They truly want to do God's will, walk in his narrow path of righteousness, and stay in it while they are in the flesh.

THOUGHTS

A VERY EXCITING BOOK! ENJOYED READING ALL THE MOVING EVENTS. EASY READING. A WONDERFUL BOOK ABOUT HAVING FAITH IN THE LORD.

BARBARA SMITH

THIS BOOK IS A LIFE LIKE DEPICTION OF GOD'S POWER TO RESTORE WHAT SATAN HAS SOUGHT TO DESTROY. IT ALSO DEMONSTRATES THAT CHRISTIANS ARE BLESSED BUT ALSO NEED TO KNOW HOW TO FIGHT SATAN.

BETTY WEST

THANK YOU FOR SHARING YOUR LATEST BOOK WITH ME. I'VE ENJOYED THE CHARACTER DEVELOPMENT THROUGHOUT THE YEARS. YOU ARE SO EFFECTIVE AT DEMONSTRATING AND COMMUNICATING GOD'S PROVISION. NOW I MUST WAIT TO SEE WHAT HAPPENS WITH CALEB AND MARY RUTH'S SHOW THAT SATAN WANTS OFF THE AIR.

JULIA CHRISTIAN

THE CHRONICLES OF CALEB AND MARY RUTH (SERIES)

We Will Always Have Faith

THE CHRONICLES OF CALEBE AND MARY RUTH

Barbara L. Wylie Apicella

authorHOUSE®

AuthorHouse™
1663 Liberty Drive
Bloomington, IN 47403
www.authorhouse.com
Phone: 1-800-839-8640

First published by AuthorHouse 10/12/2011

ISBN: 978-1-4634-7463-8 (sc)
ISBN: 978-1-4634-7462-1 (hc)
ISBN: 978-1-4634-7461-4 (e)

Library of Congress Control Number: 2011916133

Printed in the United States of America

Any people depicted in stock imagery provided by Thinkstock are models, and such images are being used for illustrative purposes only. Certain stock imagery © Thinkstock.

This book is printed on acid-free paper.

Because of the dynamic nature of the Internet, any web addresses or links contained in this book may have changed since publication and may no longer be valid. The views expressed in this work are solely those of the author and do not necessarily reflect the views of the publisher, and the publisher hereby disclaims any responsibility for them.

ACKNOWLEDGEMENT

I truly thank the Lord for being with me and helping me. I pray that this series of books bring more people to Him and helps them understand some of the things that happen in life and to love and have complete faith in the Lord. If you do, He will lead you, guide you, and help you in all your problems and needs. Read the Bible, go to Bible studies, and understand it. Have love and faith in God, the Father, Jesus Christ, His Son, and the Holy Spirit.

Chapter 1

Sandy was crying so much. When she heard something say, "I got you now." She became hysterical. Len shook her and said, "Sandy, calm down, just tell me the truth!"

She tried her best to calm down but the tears kept coming out of her eyes. Len took her over to the couch and had her sit down. He gave her some tissues and she blew her nose.

She said, "Okay Len, I will tell you what really happened. One night while you were working the second shift, I decided to go for a walk down by the lake. It was still light outside and I thought I would just go for about half an hour, what happened was; I walked a little too far. I looked up and saw that the sun had set and it was quickly starting to get dark. I started running, tripped on something, and fell down. I really hurt my ankle. When I stood up, I could hardly walk."

Len then said, "I remember the time I was with you on a date and you could hardly walk. Is that the time you're talking about?"

"Yes, and I wish that was all that happened! As I limped along the path, a white sports car was driving by. It pulled over to where I was walking and a tall man got out. He came over to me and asked me if I was all right. I said, Yes, I'm fine; I just fell and hurt my ankle. I'm on my way home now. He said, I'll be glad to take you there in my car. I said to him, That's okay, I can make it. Then he said, No, I insist on driving you home! He put his arm around my back and helped me into his car.

I did not want to do that, but he seemed so nice and wanted to help me. He got in the car and asked me where I lived. I told him my address and he started driving down the street. When we came to Louisiana Avenue, he didn't turn, but kept going straight.

I said, Wait, you just passed my street. He didn't even look at me, he

1

just kept on driving. All of a sudden, he pulled off the road into a bunch of trees. He pulled in far enough that we couldn't be seen, and then he jumped out of the car. I didn't know what he was going to do.

He grabbed the door where I was and pulled me out. I tried to fight him, but he knocked me on the ground, lifted my skirt and pulled my underware off. He then unzipped his pants, pulled them down, and jumped on me. He pulled my legs apart and started having sex with me. I was crying. You know that I was a virgin! I was in shock and so much pain!

After several minutes, he finished, jumped up, and said, Thanks a lot, I needed that. He jumped in his car and took off. I was still laying there in shock. I knew I had to get going home or my parents would be worried about me. As I limped home, I thought, I'm not going to tell my parents what happened. They will get so upset, and I didn't want you to find out because I was afraid that you would stop loving me!

I said to myself, I'll be all right; I'll just not say anything to anyone and forget it myself.

When I finally got home, my mom was looking out the window for me. When I entered, my mom and dad ran up and hugged me. Mom told me that they were just about ready to come looking for me. They saw that I had been crying, and I explained how I tripped and hurt my ankle. That is why it took me so long to get home. They looked at my ankle and saw that it was swollen.

I told them that I was sure that it wasn't broken because I was able to move it. Mom gave me an aspirin, wrapped my ankle, and helped me up the steps to my bedroom.

She said, let me help you put on your pajamas. I said, Mom, I can do it, I'm fine. I just want to go to bed. She smiled and said, Okay. If you need another aspirin, just call me and I'll get you one. She kissed me goodnight and I shut the door.

I then thought, Thank Heaven she didn't insist on taking my clothes off. She would have seen that my underpants were ripped and full of blood from me being raped by that horrible man. I decided again to completely forget about it. I went into the bathroom and kept washing myself. I hid my underpants and next time I go out, I would throw them away.

I got in bed, but I didn't sleep very much. Everytime I fell asleep, I dreamed about what happened and instantly woke up and cried again. Finally, morning came and I went down for breakfast.

Dad asked how my ankle was feeling. I told him that it was getting better already. I think it will be as good as new in a couple of days.

Around 10 o'clock that day, you called me and asked if I would like to go to the beach. I don't know if you remember, but I told you about my ankle."

Len was sitting in shock while he was hearing this story. He said, "Yes, I remember taking you to lunch instead and how strange you were acting. Sandy, you should have had your parents call the police, we probably could have found that man and arrested him. There weren't very many sport cars around here back then."

Sandy was crying again. She said, "Len, I loved you and I was afraid if you knew what happened to me, you wouldn't want any thing to do with me, being I was raped."

Len hugged her and said, "Sandy, I loved you so much and knew I always would, no matter what ever happened. Sandy, it wasn't your fault! I still love you and will forever, but I still don't understand why you don't want any kids!"

Sandy started crying even more. She said, "Let me finish the rest of the story and you'll understand."

Len replied, "Come to think of it, you were acting strangely and I asked you why. You kept telling me that nothing was wrong."

"I was trying to forget about being raped, but it wasn't working out. I know I was acting weird. Even my mom and dad asked me what was going on and I told them the same thing I told you, that nothing was wrong. Two weeks later my period was due. It never came, and then I was worried. I though, Maybe it's just late, so I waited two more weeks. It still had not come. I was upset. I didn't know what I should do.

I called my sister, Judy, told her what had happened to me and that I never told anyone else. Now I haven't gotten my period. She told me to go to either Kissimmee or Orlando, see a GYN doctor, and have him test me to see if I was pregnant. If I wasn't pregnant, just try to put what happened completely out of my mind. If I was pregnant, I could move up to her house in Georgia if I didn't want anyone down here to know. We hung up and I made an appointment with a doctor in Orlando. Two days later, I went up and had my blood drawn. He said he would let me know the results in around three days.

When I got home, I was so upset and worried. I didn't even know who the father was, and I was trying to decide what I should do if I was pregnant. Three days later, I got a phone call from the doctor's nurse. She said, Congradulations, you are around one month pregnant and will have the baby in eight months. Now I was really in shock! I called my sister and told her the results. She told me that the decision was entirely up to me. My sister was married a year and a half, but still had not gotten pregnant yet.

I asked her if I could stay with them while I was pregnant until I decided what to do. In no way was I going to have an abortion and kill the baby! That is truly against God's will! I would either have to keep the baby or give it up for adoption. My sister and her husband promised they would not ever tell anyone what happened. to me.

Later that day, I told my mom and dad that I was going to go up to Georgia and live with Judy and her husband for a while. I could probably find a good job there. My mom and dad were shocked. My dad asked me what my sister had to say about it. I told him that she said that I was welcomed to stay with them as long as I wanted to. Then my mom asked me when I planned to leave. I said that I was leaving tomorrow morning. I'm going upstairs right now to pack my clothes and I asked them to wish me luck. My parents looked at each other and tears started running down their faces.

My mom said that they would miss me so much. We love you, you are our baby girl! I hugged them and told them not to worry, that I would be back some day. I said, By the way, don't let Len know that I am leaving until after I'm gone. I'll try to keep in touch with all of you. The next morning, I kissed them goodbye and left for Georgia."

Len said, "I remember when you left! I drove over to your house that morning to see you. Your mom answered the door and looked like she had been crying. I asked if you were home and she told me that you had gone to live with your sister in Georgia. I couldn't believe my ears! I asked her why. She never said anything about that to me.

I told her that you were acting strange for the past month, that you didn't want me to kiss, or even touch you. Maybe she just doesn't want to be with me anymore for some reason!

Your mom told me that she had no idea why you left, but you were also acting strangely to them. I told your mom to please ask you to call me so we can talk about what's really going on.

Your mom told me that she would and that she was also going to call Judy and ask her why you're coming up to stay with her.

I was so upset and sad. I missed you already and couldn't figure out what was going on. I loved you so much! I knew that I would always love you no matter what, but apparently you didn't know that."

Sandy said, "I wish I had known that, but I didn't and was trying to make the right decision, whether to keep the baby or not. When I finally got to my sister's home, she and her husband told me that they would help me anyway they can She gave me the name of a GYN doctor she knew and I made an appointment.

I did fine with my pregnancy, but I made sure that I wasn't around when my mom and dad came up to visit. I didn't call you because I figured that by now you probably had another girlfriend."

"Why would you ever think that? Why didn't you know how much I loved you? I never even dated anyone while you were gone," Len cried.

"I'm so sorry! I also loved you so much, but because of what happened I was afraid you wouldn't have loved me anymore."

"Okay, there's nothing we can do about it now. Go on with your story."

"The funny part is, when I was there two months, my sister found out that she was pregnant. I was due in October and she was due in January. Now that we were both pregnant, we were going to the same doctor and both doing well. I finally made the decision to give my baby up for adoption. I prayed that my baby would be given to wonderful people and have a great life.

I felt that God would be with the baby. I prayed for the baby to have a better life than it could with me. On October 14th , I started having pain and my sister took me to the hospital. The doctor came and checked me. He told me that I would be having the baby in the next few hours. They gave me a shot in my arm and I fell asleep.

Hours later, I had my baby. I woke up in a bed in a hospital room. I checked my abdomen and noticed that the baby wasn't there. I started crying! My sister was sitting aside of me. I asked her, Did I have my baby? Judy said, Yes, about an hour ago. Just then, a nurse came into the room. I asked her if I had a boy or a girl. She said, I'm sorry, aren't you giving the baby up for adoption?

I said, Yes, but can I please see my baby? The nurse said, No, your not allowed to see the baby if your giving it up . I really started crying then! My sister and the nurse both hugged me, my sister was crying too. The nurse said, I'm so sorry, but there is nothing I can do, but I will tell you that you had a 6.5 pound baby boy, 21 inches long and he is doing fine. Please don't tell anyone that I told you this or I'll be in trouble.

Thank you for telling me. I still wish that I could see my son. Does he look like me or someone else?

The nurse said, I'm sorry, I told you more than I should have already.

I said, Don't worry, my sister and I won't tell anyone what you told us.

Len, I'm telling you this because I want you to know what I had. That was over ten years ago. So now, he will be eleven years old on October 14. I pray for him everyday that he is doing fine and having a good life."

Len smiled and said, "I will also pray for him everyday, now that I know about his birth. I wish you had let me and your parents know what happened. I might have gotten upset when I first heard about it, but I would have still married you and raised the baby. I'm sure that your parents would have also been shocked, but they would love a child that is part of you. Thank the Lord that you didn't have an abortion!"

"I'm truly sorry that I didn't keep the baby. I miss him and love him so much! Please don't tell my parents or anyone else what happened."

"Don't worry, I won't say anything about it, but now that I know and told you how I felt, would you please have a child with me, which we both can love and take care of?"

Sandy hugged Len and said, "Thank you, I love you so much, I will never take those pills again and we will have our child." They kissed each other and thanked the Lord for being with them.

Chapter 2

Caleb and Mary Ruth were doing fine and had their great friends with them to help others. Tammy, Pepi, Mike, and Raymond were helping them so much. They were now traveling around the state whenever they were able to and teaching the Bible. Caleb and Mary Ruth's grandparents were always giving them money and supporting them. They were so very thankful for that but knew they couldn't do it forever.

One day Mary Ruth and Mike were teaching some young people that had only been in class for two weeks. They always started teaching them in Genesis, how God created heaven and earth on the first day. Then continued to teach them about what he did in the next six days. This was their 4th study. After the Bible study, a young girl, named Roseanne, came up to them.

She smiled and said, "You both are wonderful teachers. I am learning so much in this small amount of time. I never realized what a lot of the verses really meant. Thank God I came here! I feel that I am getting so much closer to the Lord already and am so thankful!"

Mike smiled and said, "We are so thankful that you and the others came to learn from the Bible. It makes you stronger Christians to understand what the Bible means. Some day you can also help others and live in righteousness."

"I wanted to tell you that my mom and dad have a radio station and I was wondering if maybe you and your other teachers would like to teach on the radio."

Mary Ruth and Mike hugged her and Mary Ruth said, "Of course we would! We are all 100% with the Lord and my brother Caleb is nearly finished his Christian College."

"I first have to ask my parents if it would be alright, but they were the ones who told me to come to your Bible study."

They hugged each other again, and Roseann said, "I will let you know ASAP if it's okay with mom and dad. I have to go now. Bye."

"Oh, how wonderful this will be if it happens! I know the Lord is leading us. I can't wait to tell Caleb, Tammy, Pepi and Raymond! They will be so excited! They're all at my house now."

Mike laughed and said, "They'll be as excited as we are!" He then hugged Mary Ruth again and kissed her.

She was surprised! She did have some feelings for Mike, but didn't think that he even cared about her. She smiled at him and they kissed again.

He smiled at her and said, "You are the most beautiful, wonderful, girl in the world and the best thing about you is your belief in the Lord and how your brother, Caleb, Tammy, and Paul brought me to Him! I am so very thankful. I love you all, but I love you in another way also. I know I have been a bad person for a long time, but believe me, I have completely changed."

"I know, Mike. We had been trying to help you for a long time. The time had finally come and the Lord brought you to Him."

"Yes, but I'm so sorry for the sins I had committed and for hurting people, especially you!"

"Don't ever worry about what you did to me. I'm fine. It was worth breaking a bone to bring you to out Lord and Savior. Your sins were forgiven! Now you must do your best never to sin, love everyone, be kind and help others."

"Believe me, I truly trust in the Lord, pray that I can do His will, and walk in His narrow path of righteousness."

"Don't forget, Satan can still get into your mind and try to get you upset or worried and do wrong. You must always have complete faith in the Lord that He will take care of you. Remember how Len had complete faith for five years, then he was healed by the Lord."

Mike said, "Yes, that was so very wonderful!"

"Come on, let's go over to my house and tell everyone the great news." They jumped in the car and went to Mary Ruth's.

They got there and went in the front door. Her grandparents were watching TV. Mary Ruth ran over, hugged them, and asked, "Are the others in our group still all out on the back porch?"

Thelma said, "Yes, their making plans on how to lead more people to the Lord."

Mike smiled and said, "You and your husband come out with us. We have something wonderful to tell you all."

Thelma and Tom jumped up. Tom said, "We can't wait to hear what the good news is!"

They all went out on the back porch and said hello to everyone. Caleb asked, "How was your Bible study?"

"It was great, and something great might be happening!" said Mike. "Mary Ruth will tell you all what happened."

Tammy smiled and said, "I hope it is wonderful, because we truly need some help to bring more people to Jesus."

"First of all, we're not 100% sure that this will happen, but we will find out soon. We have a girl in our Bible study class, named Roseanne. When the study was over, she came over to us and really thrilled us. She told us that her parents owned a radio station and she is going to ask them if we can do our great teaching on it!" cried Mary Ruth.

Everyone jumped up and hugged each other. "That's just what we were discussing before you and Mike came in. We were trying to figure out how we could be with more and more people and bring them to our Lord. I sure hope it happens! Let us pray." They all held hands, Caleb said,

"DEAR GOD, WE PRAY THAT WE CAN TEACH MANY PEOPLE ON THE RADIO ABOUT YOUR SON, JESUS CHRIST, OUR LORD AND SAVIOR. IF THEY REPENT OF THEIR SINS AND ACCEPT HIM, THEIR SINS WILL BE FORGIVEN AND THEY CAN ALSO COME TO HIS FATHER, GOD, THROUGH HIM. THEY WILL ALSO GO TO HEAVEN SPIRTUALLY AFTER THEY LEAVE THEIR FLESH FULL LIFE. WE THANK YOU AND LOVE YOU SO FOR HELPING AND LEADING US TO DO YOUR WILL. WE PROMISE WE ALWAYS WILL! IN JESUS HOLY NAME, AMEN"

They all hugged each other again, espically Caleb and Tammy, Mary Ruth and Mike. The others did feel that they all loved each other and were becoming closer and closer.

As Mary Ruth's friends were hearing about what happened, Roseanne had gotten home. Her parents were in the kitchen getting ready for supper.

She said, "Hi, mom and dad. I was at the very great Bible study that you suggested that I go to. I know that it was only the forth time I was there, but it was really great the way Mary Ruth and Mike explained versus in the Bible. It was wonderful! I learned so much. It is amazing! I know that I had already read the Bible before, but I never really understood what a lot of the versus meant. I just wondered about things. Now, I don't have to wonder. They are so smart and explain everything. We're even allowed to ask questions, if we still don't completely understand."

Mom said, "That's really great, I wonder if older people are allowed to attend the Bible studies or is it just for the young?"

"I'm sure anyone can attend. The teachers love everyone, no matter what their age, and they want to bring everyone to the Lord."

Roseanne's dad said, "That is so great! I'm glad that you are going there! We have heard that they were wonderful teachers, even though they are young."

"I was talking to Mary Ruth and Mike after the study and told them how great they taught everything. I hope you and dad don't get mad, but I told them that you owned a radio station and maybe they can teach on it. They hopefully will get people to listen," replied Roseanne.

Her dad smiled and said, "That's a good idea, but I have to charge people for the time they're on the radio. That's how we make our money. Do you think they can pay for an hour or maybe a half hour?"

"I don't know if they can. I told them that I would call and tell them what you said, after I talk to you. I guess I didn't even think about the cost."

She called Mary Ruth and told her the circumstances and what it would cost. Mary Ruth was sad to hear this and said, "There is no way we can pay for the radio and we won't ask our grandparents for the money. They have given us so much already."

"I'm so sorry that I even mentioned the radio station. I never even thought about the cost."

"Thank you anyway. I'm sure something will happen to help our teachings someday. We all have complete faith in the Lord. We always did and always will! See you next week at our Bible study."

Mary Ruth hung up the phone and went out to the back porch. Everyone was still talking about what they will teach on the radio.

Mary Ruth came in and everyone could see how sad she looked. They just looked at her.

"What's wrong, Mary Ruth?" asked Mike.

She told them that Roseann was on the phone and that she apologized for mentioning the radio station to me and Mike. She talked to her parents and her dad told her that people had to pay money to be on the radio. She said she never even thought about that. I told her not to be upset, that the Lord would lead us somewhere and help us."

Mike ran to Mary Ruth and hugged her. He said, "Don't be upset Mary Ruth, what you said about the Lord is true and will happen. We all have faith in Him and things will work out for us."

Caleb said, "Let's just forget about what happened and know that something will happen, some way, where we can reach more and more people. Let's all try to think of some thing that we might be able to do."

Meanwhile, Roseann sat down at the table with her mom and dad. Mom asked, "Can I get you something to eat?"

"No thank you. I'm not hungry." Suddenly, she started crying.

"Roseann, what's wrong?" asked her dad.

"I'm just so sorry that I told Mary Ruth and Mike about your radio station. I forgot about people having to pay for it. I feel like slapping myself! I hope they're not mad at me."

"I'm sure they're not mad. They love everyone," replied her mom.

Her dad held her hand and said, "Roseann, I have an idea! How about I let them have an hour a day for two weeks. I just remembered that one of my renters will be finished at the end of next week. The time is very early in the morning at 6AM. I won't charge them anything if they want to just try it for two weeks.

Roseann smiled and said, "At least I can tell them that they can have two weeks free! It might help them, at least a little!" She jumped up and ran to the phone to call Mary Ruth again.

They were all still sitting on the porch trying to think of something, when they heard the phone ringing again. Thelma came to the door and said, "Mary Ruth, its Roseann. She would like to talk to you again."

Mary Ruth went in, picked up the phone and said, "Hello."

"I just want to tell you that my dad will soon be having someone leave his station and he has not gotten anyone yet to fill that time in. He is offering you and your group one hour a day, at 6 Am, for two weeks, and he won't charge you anything. What do you think? Would you like just two weeks?"

Mary Ruth was stunned! She said, "We will be so glad for two free weeks on a radio! That is so wonderful! Please thank your dad for us."

"I'm so happy for all of you and I can't wait to listen to you all on the radio before I go to school in the morning. I will tell everyone at my school about it. I'll also talk to my dad and let you know the exact dates and we'll make an arrangement for you all to come over to see my dad so he can tell you exactly how to do everything."

"Thank you so much, Roseann! I can't wait to tell my group about this." They hung up the phone and Mary Ruth ran out to the back porch.

"Guess what! Roseann's dad is going to give us two free weeks on the radio! One hour a day at 6 AM. It won't be very long from now. Roseann is going to let me know the dates."

Everyone jumped up and cried "Thank the Lord!"

Caleb said, "We have to decide what we're going to teach. We need to get into the people that listen to us very quickly as we will only have two weeks to help them understand. It's a great start for us and maybe someday we can do more."

They all held hands and thanked the Lord so much that this was going to happen. They asked Him to please help them do the right things. They then sat down and talked for quite awhile. Caleb ran in and told his grandparents what was going to happen.

Thelma said, "Wow, that is so great, and its going to be free!" Caleb then explained the whole thing to them.

"How wonderful! I'm going to tell everyone I know about this. Everyone will want to get up early and hear your teaching of the Lord," exclaimed Tom. "By the way, what are you going to be teaching about specifically since you all only have two weeks?"

"That's what we're trying to decide right now. I think we're going to explain how to have faith in Jesus and be thankful for what He did for us on the cross. We're also going to say certain versus of Matthew, Mark, Luke, and John from the Bible and explain what they mean. We will be so happy to have many people understand the Bible, God the

Father, Jesus, His Son, and the Holy Spirit. I have to go back out now, we're making notes, and every one of us will do some teaching."

Caleb went back to the porch and sat down. Tammy said, "We're so excited!" We know the Lord will help us say the right things."

"I would like to talk about Paul and how he became a disciple. I feel like, in a way, I started out somewhat like him. I then came completely to the Lord because of Pepi being put in the prison cell with me." stated Raymond.

Mike said, "I also know that I became a Christian, although I was not a very good person to start with. Thanks to Tammy, Caleb, and their friend, Paul."

"I was just a nobody, but thanks to Caleb and Mary Ruth, I completely changed," said Pepi.

"Mary Ruth, Tammy, and I have been through a lot in our life, but we had great faith in the Lord, and He always saved us. We know that we're going to meet our destiny because we stay faithful to Him. That is the greatest gift there is, to love the Lord and have the Holy Spirit in your body helping you. I know we all have the Holy Spirit because we all are true believers in Christ and what He did for us on the cross. Our goal is to have people understand the Lord and come to Him. That really is the greatest thing people can do."

Mary Ruth said, "I wish we had more than two weeks. There is so very much to teach people about the Bible and have them understand and follow what it says."

"Also, they need to know that one day, the Lord, Jesus will be coming back to us, but before He comes, an antichrist will come and pretend to be the Lord. There's a lot to learn. I know the Lord helps us so we can serve Him and bring more people to Him," replied Tammy.

"We did write some good things. We have to get together every night and practice. It's getting late now, we can meet here again tomorrow about 7PM, okay?" asked Caleb.

They all hugged each other, said, "Bye." They were so very happy.

Chapter 3

The next day, Roseann called and told Mary Ruth the dates that they would have. They could come over to the station on Saturday morning, her dad would explain everything to them and exactly what they need to do in their hour.

That night Mary Ruth told their group about Saturday. They decided to all meet at Caleb and Mary Ruth's home and go together.

Saturday came and they went to the radio station and met Roseann's dad, Daniel. They all thanked him so much for giving them two weeks free.

He showed them where they would be sitting, the microphones, and so on. How they needed to talk and do their best. He also said that people would be listening to them in their homes, in their cars, and on portable radios. Remember that they will be young, middle aged, and old people, Christians, and other people of different religions. Be careful of condemning other people.

Tammy said, "Don't worry; we're just going to teach the Bible. We aren't going to hurt anyone. We love everyone!"

After talking for awhile, Daniel wished them good luck. They went back to Caleb and Mary Ruth's home, sat down, and talked. After awhile, the others in the group went home and they would all meet again tomorrow.

Caleb said, "I am so thankful that this is taking place so early in the morning and I can still go to college every day."

They got up and went to the kitchen for lunch. Their grandparents were there and Mary Ruth told them their dates for the two weeks on the radio.

"If you need any help at all, please let us know. We'll be more than happy to help you," said Thelma.

"We know how you and grandpa love us. We love you both too," replied Caleb.

Mary Ruth then said to Caleb, "Let's go over and tell Sandy and Len the good news. I'm sure they'll be happy to hear it!"

"That's a good idea, I just hope their home," said Caleb.

After lunch they walked over to Sandy and Len's house. The cars were in the driveway, so they assumed they were home. They knocked on the door, waited a couple of minutes and tried again. No one answered.

Caleb said, "I guess they went for a walk or something." As they started to leave, Len opened the door. When he saw Caleb and Mary Ruth, he ran out and hugged them.

"Come on in, Sandy and I were just taking a nap. I'm so glad to see you both." They entered the house and saw Sandy coming down the stairs. They ran over, hugged and kissed her.

Sandy said, "Oh, I'm so glad to see you! Unfortunally, we don't see each other now as much as we used to. Len and I both work, Caleb is at college, and Mary Ruth just graduated from high school. Also I know you both have been teaching your great Bible studies. We're so glad you came over today."

Caleb said, "We're so sorry we woke you up from your nap, but we have great news to tell you!" They went and sat down in the living room. Mary Ruth told them about their Bible study going to be on the radio for two weeks.

Len said, "That is so great! Did you decide what you are going to teach?"

"Since we only have two weeks, we're mainly going to talk about Jesus and what He has done for us. We definitely want to have others understand and accept Jesus as their Lord and Savior. We will give them our phone number if they would like to learn a lot more about the Bible. We will also tell them that even after you become a Christian, you still need to read the Bible, understand it, and obey God."

"Yes, some people who are Christians only go to church on Sunday, which is nice, but Christains need to do what the Lord tells them in the Bible. We pray that it works out well!"

Sandy said, "We will also pray for both of you, Tammy, Pepi, Mike and Raymond to do well."

"We just about have it all set up. It won't be long until we start," replied Caleb.

"6 AM is a great time for us, since I'm also working day shift right now. We can't wait!" said Len.

Mary Ruth asked, "How are you two doing?" Sandy and Len just looked at each other.

Caleb said, "I can see that something is going on in your life. Do you want to tell us about it?"

"We had a big problem, but everything is okay now," replied Len.

"If you ever need us to help you in any way, let us know. We love you both and pray for you to have a great life. In fact, by now we thought you would have one or two babies," said Mary Ruth.

Len laughed and said, "Don't worry, we keep trying and I'm sure it will happen someday." Sandy smiled and hugged him, but for some reason, both Caleb and Mary Ruth thought that she forced the smile. They stayed and talked for a while, then went home.

Caleb said, "I have a feeling that something did happen in their life that they don't want to talk about. We will start praying for them that everything will turn out all right."

Sandy and Len were eating supper and Sandy said, "Isn't it strange that Mary Ruth mentioned about us having babies? I feel so bad for what happened to me and not keeping my baby."

"Sandy, some day we will have a child. I just pray that your child is doing fine."

"Next week, I'm going to a GYN doctor just to be checked out. I figured that I would get pregnant right away but I didn't." On Tuesday she went to the doctor, was checked, and told that she was fine and wouldn't have a problem getting pregnant. She was so happy! She went back to work and told Len the good news. He also was so happy!

Chapter 4

Very soon, the first day of the radio Bible teaching came on a Monday. The first thing Caleb did was introduce everyone and explained to the listeners that they would only be on for two weeks. Mainly because they could not afford to pay for it. He also told them how grateful they were that the owner of the radio station was giving these two weeks to them.

Roseann's dad, Daniel Johnson, was sitting with them. He told the people why he did this for them. "Although they are young, they understand the Bible and are able to explain it to others and bring them to accept the Lord and Savior, Jesus Christ, as I and my family do."

Caleb then began the teaching from the book of John, in the New Testament. For the next two weeks, the whole group taught. They had no idea how many people were listening to them. When the two weeks were over, they again thanked Daniel.

Mary Ruth said, "We loved teaching on the radio, but we have no idea if anyone listened."

"I'm sure many people were listening. If anyone calls, I'll be glad to give him or her your phone number, if they would like to come and learn more at your Bible studies."

They all hugged and thanked Daniel again and went to Caleb amd Mary Ruth's home. They were so happy and grateful for what happened but they were also sad that it was over already.

Tammy said, "Let's thank God for the two wonderful weeks and be totally grateful and happy."

"Yes, and we will always keep our faith in the Lord and believe that he will lead us all to our destiny, which I know is to do His will," said Caleb.

Several days later, Thelma's phone rang while they were eating breakfast. She picked it up and said, "Hello." The man said, "Hi, this is

Daniel Johnson, the owner of the radio station. Is Caleb or Mary Ruth there? I'd like to speak to one of them."

"Just a minute please, also thank you ever so much for helping them like you did." She waved at the grandchildren and Caleb came over and picked up the phone.

"Hi, this is Caleb."

"Hi Caleb, this is Daniel. I just wanted to give you some great news. In the last few days, many people called and asked what happened to you and your group. They all loved your teaching. A lot of them missed the first day and didn't realize that you would only be here for two weeks. I told them that I would give them your phone number so they could come to your Bible studies since you couldn't afford to be on the radio. Most of them said, We work and have many other things to do, we can't attend Bible studies. We like hearing it on the radio in the morning before we go to work, our kids like it too. We all are going to send you money so they could afford to come back and be on the radio."

"Wow, I'm so glad that some people liked us!"

Daniel said, "So, many, many people said the same thing and now more and more money is pouring in to me for you and your group. I'm sure that they will continue to help you. They truly love what you all taught them and want to learn more. I talked to the man who took the 6AM time over and he said that he would be glad to change his time so you and your group could return. In fact, he said that he wants to listen to your teaching also. Well, what do you think? Will you come back?"

Caleb shouted, "Of course we will! We are so happy and definitely will do our best!"

"I know you will. You can start again next Monday and I'm also going to make announcements on the radio to let all the people know that you all will be back again at 6 AM. So many people donated to you! More than likely they will keep it up. We'll see you about 5:30 AM on Monday."

"Thank you ever so much! See you soon! Bye, bye!" He hung up the phone and ran into the kitchen. He told Mary Ruth and his grandparents what was happening. They all hugged each other, thanked and praised the Lord for what he had done for them.

Tom said, "I'm so glad all those people sent money for your group. Thelma and I will also donate and will tell others to listen to you all and support you."

That evening, when the others arrived, Caleb and Mary Ruth told them the great news. They all thanked the Lord and prayed that He would help them teach the right things and help all others that are in need.

Mike said, "Hopefully in the future we can start a wonderful Christian ministrey and help all the poor, needy, and helpless people, teach them about the Lord and bring them to the Him!"

"That would be so very wonderful! I'm so thankful also that He brought you, Tammy, Pepi, and Raymond to Caleb and me," said May Ruth.

They started getting the new lessons made. Caleb was the main teacher and he had a lot of help and decisions from Mary Ruth and Tammy and great teachings from his entire group.

When Monday came, the first thing they did was thank all the people for donating to them so they were able to come back and told them that because of their donations, they will be able to help many others come to the Lord and become good Christian people.

The first thing they always did was pray to God and thank Him for their teachings. At the end, they would again thank God and ask him to bless the people that were listening. They then started their new series from the book of Matthew. They began to have people understand about God's Son, Jesus Christ. He came to the world to save us from our sin because He loves us, wants to help us understand how to live, do His will, and walk in His path of righteousness. Love your neighbors as you love yourself. Be kind and help those in need. You will learn more and more how the Lord wants you to live. Take the time to keep yourself spiritually fit. Spiritual exercise will not only help in your life, but in the next life also. Take time with God everyday, quiet time for reading the Bible and prayer.

More and more teachings went by, some of the things they taught were, always put God first in your life. If you can, get together with other believers and make plans to do good for poor and helpless people.

They always gave their phone number and address if anyone wanted to talk with them. The Lord led and guided the group to teach well, so that even children could understand the teaching. They had great amounts of money sent to them and were able to keep teaching. Caleb also graduated from his Bible college.

Many months had gone by, Sandy and Len loved listening to Caleb,

Mary Ruth and their group every morning. It was so amazing how all these young people understood and taught the Bible. It had to bring many people to Jesus.

Sandy still had not gotten pregnant. Len said, "Sandy, I know that you aren't taking those pills anymore and the doctor checked you out. I think I should also be checked. What do you think?"

"I don't think anything is wrong with you, but if you want to be checked, I'll make an appointment for you."

A few days later he went to the doctor. On Friday he went back for the results. The doctor said, "I'm really sorry to say this, but your sperm is extremally low for some reason. There is only a very small chance that you will ever get your wife pregnant."

Len was so very sad. He didn't want to tell Sandy, but he had no choice. The work day was just about over when he got back to the police station.

Sandy saw him, jumped up, and ran over to him. She was smiling and hoping to hear good news until she looked at his face. Tears were coming from his eyes. "Len, what's wrong?"

He told her the results and she started crying too. She said, "Len, don't worry and think negatively. We must think positive and have faith that the Lord will bring us a child."

"You're right, I do believe so much in the Lord, look how He has helped me with my physical problem and how He had helped us all when we were on the island. He helped us in so very many ways. He kept the plane from crashing, He helped me and Tom rescue Caleb and Mary Ruth from the factory. He helped us when the theater caved in and how He took care of Caleb and Mary Ruth their whole life and still does. He leads and guides them to meet their destiny because they are completely faithful. The Lord has also brought others to them."

"It's amazing how the Lord helps us because of our belief and faith we have in Him. We do out best to completely obey Him also. We will pray to the Lord every day and know that He will someday give us a child, if that is His will for us."

Chapter 5

One afternoon, the phone rang. Mary Ruth answered it. It was a woman, named Ellen, from Georgia. She was crying.

Mary Ruth asked, "Whats wrong, Ellen!"

"I'm so sad. I live in Atlanta, Georgia. I listen to you and your group every morning and I love your teaching so much. I attend a loving Baptist Church and I also love it. I am so sad because the minister and his wife were both shot and killed when some crazy man broke into their home."

Mary Ruth said, "Oh no, that is so very sad! My parents were killed in our home. My dad was also a pastor. We had wonderful parents and we were young children when it happened. Fortunally, Caleb and I escaped."

"Luckily, their child, was not there when it happened. He was staying at a friends. He's ten years old, their only child, which they adopted right after he was born. The other sad part is that they don't have any relatives. Their son, Matthew, has to be put in a state orphanage. We all want to take care of him, but the state says he has to go to the orphanage first, because he has no relatives. Please pray for him!"

"Of course we will! We will ask everyone to pray for him!"

"Thank you so much! I love you and your group. I'm feeling better all of a sudden for some reason. Bye, bye."

Mary Ruth hung up the phone as some thoughts entered her mind. She went to Caleb and told him what just happened. He got the same thoughts in his mind. He said, "Come on Mary Ruth, for some reason we have to go over and tell this to Sandy and Len." They jumped in the car, drove over, and knocked on the door.

Sandy came to the door, smiled, hugged them, and said, "Come on in, we were just setting here watching television."

They hugged Len and said, "Hello." As they sat down, the world news was on. It started talking about the pastor and his wife that were killed in Atlanta, Georgia. It didn't mention anything about their son.

Sandy said, "Oh, how sad that someone would kill a pastor and his wife!"

"Do you remember when we told you what happened to our parents and how Satan wanted to do away with us also, because he knew that we had a great destiny with God, but we got away. He kept trying to get rid of us, but the Lord always saved us. I believe we are starting to do our destiny now," said Mary Ruth.

"Of course we remember that! Do you think an evil man of Satan killed the pastor and his wife?" asked Len.

"Yes, we think that might be why they were killed, but the thing is, the television news didn't say anything about a child they have," stated Caleb.

Sandy replied, "Maybe they didn't have any children."

"A little while ago, I got a phone call from a woman, named Ellen, who always listens to our teachings. It was her pastor and his wife from a Bapist church that were killed. She also told me about their son, Matthew, who was at a friends house when this happened," said Mary Ruth.

Len asked, "Do you think that he might also have a destiny like you both do?"

"Yes. It might be. If it is true, we need to help him in case someone tries to get rid of him."

"That's a good idea. Do you want us to help you in some way? We'll do as much as we can, but you know that we both work."

"We want to tell you something else about the child. We were both told by God to do this. The woman who called me said the boy was ten years old and he was adopted in Georgia by the pastor and his wife when he was just a new born baby."

Sandy jumped up and said, "Do you think this could be my son!!!! I know I didn't tell you what happened to me, but I know the Lord knows. That's why He sent you over, to tell us!"

Len cried, "What if Matthew is your son! Even if he isn't, we have to save that little boy! Caleb, can you and Mary Ruth come to Georgia with us and help us find him?"

"Of course! The others in our group will do the teaching while we're gone."

"I'm going to call Captian Hardy and tell him that Sandy and I can't come to work tomorrow and maybe for a few more days. I will tell him the reason why. I know he will understand. We'll leave first thing in the morning. Just pack a few things that you will need. We'll pick you up at 6AM. We will arrive there around 2 PM and go right to the police department."

The next day they arrived in Atlanta and went into the police station. Len asked if they could please speak to Captain Wilson. The officer called the captain and he told him to bring them in. They all introduced themselves and sat down.

The captian was extremely happy to meet Caleb and Mary Ruth, as he listened to their wonderful teachings every day.

Len told him that he was a police officer from St. Cloud and Sandy also worked at the police department. He also told him that they knew Caleb and Mary Ruth for over ten years as they grew up.

"Captain Hardy called me last night and told me that you all were coming here today," said Captain Wilson.

Len said, "I love Captain Hardy. He's a great guy and always helps me." He then asked about the murder of the pastor of the Baptist church and his wife, and if they found the murderer yet.

"Not yet, but we will. We are doing everything we can to find them. Apparently, a witness saw two men run from their house."

Mary Ruth asked, "What about their son, Matthew?"

"Right now he is staying at a state orphanage in this city."

"Can we go and see him?" Caleb asked.

"Sure, it's not very far from here. I'll call them and let them know that you all are coming." He then gave them directions to find the place.

Len, Sandy, Caleb, and Mary Ruth jumped in the car and headed for the orphanage. Caleb said, "Drive as fast as you can! I feel that something is starting to happen to him."

Len pressed on the gas and they got there very quickly. They all jumped out of the car and ran in. Len told the man in charge who they are and that they were here to visit Matthew.

The man said, "I know. I just spoke to Captain Wilson on the phone. I sent someone to get him and bring him here, but we can't find him."

Sandy asked, "Would you happen to have a pitcure of him in case we would see him somewhere?"

"Of course, I'll be glad to show it to you. In fact, I can make a copy of it, but I'm sure we will find him. The kids could be playing hide and seek or some kind of game."

The man made a copy of the picture and showed the original one to them. He looked at the picture and looked at Sandy. He said, "Wow, this little boy looks a lot like you! Are you related to him? I was told that he didn't have any relatives and that's why he's here."

Sandy was in shock! She couldn't even speak. Mary Ruth said, "Thank you for showing us the picture, we'll be back in a little while and I'm sure you will have found him."

When they left, the man that worked there thought, That lady looks so much like Matthew and she didn't even say a word. I do know that the boy was adopted, Could she be his mother? I sure do hope we find Matthew or we'll really be in trouble!

Meanwhile, the lady that was looking for Matthew asked the kids if they knew where he was. One of the boys said, "We were playing in the yard and heard someone calling his name. He said that someone probably wants to tell him something, so he ran over to the fence to talk to him. All of a sudden, the big man pulled him over the fence and carried him over to a black car. We were just on our way in to tell you all what happened."

The woman cried, "Oh no!" She ran back in to tell the boss. She told him what happened and he called the police.

Meanwhile, Sandy, Len, Caleb, and Mary Ruth got in their car. Len hugged Sandy and said, "More than likely, Matthew is your son! He is so good looking, he actually looks just like you."

Tears were coming out of Sandy's eyes. She cried, "OH DEAR LORD, PLEASE, PLEASE, PLEASE, PROTECT MATTHEW LIKE YOU ALWAYS PROTECTED CALEB AND MARY RUTH." They all then held hands and prayed for him.

Len said, "Lets go take a ride around the block and see if we can see anything suspicious or maybe he just left the orphanage."

They drove out and stopped at the red light. As they were sitting there, a black car passed in front of them. Len and Sandy saw a boy in the back seat trying to break the window.

Sandy screamed, "That was my son!!!!!!!!! I know it was!!!!!!!!

Len stepped on the gas and went after the black car. He then started to beep his horn.

Caleb and Mary Ruth also saw the boy at the back window. Caleb said, "Sandy, we also saw him! Len, do something to stop that car!"

"I plan too!" crid Len. "All of you hang on!" As he was passing the black car, Len pushed the front of their car off the road.

Len and Caleb jumped out, the two men in the black car also jumped out. The one man had a gun in his hand but Caleb kicked it with his foot, the man dropped it and it rolled away. They started fighting with each other.

Sandy and Mary Ruth ran over to the black car, got Matthew and took him to their car. Sandy hugged and kissed him and said, "Don't worry, everything will be okay!"

Mary Ruth ran out of the car. She found the gun and picked it up. She fired it up in the air, to get the men's attention. They stopped fighting and Len and Caleb ran over to her.

Len grabbed the gun and said, ""Get down on your knees and put your hands up." They did what he told them.

Within the next minute, a police car drove up. Two officers jumped out of the car with guns. The one office yelled, "Drop the gun!"

Len yelled, "Those are the men that kidnapped Matthew!" He dropped the gun.

One of the men on the ground yelled, "They're lying! They kidnapped the boy and we were trying to save him! They were going to kill us!"

The officers looked at each other. They didn't know who to believe. Suddenly, they saw Sandy and Matthew get out of their car.

As they ran over to Len, Caleb, and Mary Ruth, Mary Ruth yelled, "Officers, I am Mary Ruth Powell." She pointed to her brother and said, "This is my brother Caleb Powell. We do Bible teaching on the radio every morning at 6 AM. We are not lying!"

One of the officers said, "I do listen to that teaching every morning, but how do I know for sure that you are the ones that teach?"

Len yelled, "I am a police officer from St. Cloud, Florida. We all came up here to help Matthew! We were just at the orphanage to see him and they couldn't find him anywhere."

The other man on the ground yelled. "Their all lying, don't believe a word they say!"

The officers still didn't know who to believe. Suddenly, Matthew yelled, "Please believe these people that I am with! The ones that kidnapped me are the two men kneeling down. These people here pushed the car I was in off the road to save me and these two women took me to their car as the men were fighting." Then Matthew said, "I know that the Lord has led them here to save me! Those are probably the two men who killed my parents and now they wanted me to die too. I believe Satan sent them."

Mary Ruth and Cable thought, This boy has a destiny like ours. I can feel it! Sandy and Len thought basically the same thing.

One of the officers went over and handcuffed the two men and put them in the back of their car. Then both officers went over and shook hands with Sandy, Len, Caleb, and Mary Ruth. They hugged Matthew. They thanked them for saving him.

The one officer was so happy to meet Caleb and Mary Ruth. He said, "We need you all to come back to the police station with us. We have to explain what happened to Captain Wilson. You can bring Matthew in your car."

Chapter 6

As they left, Mathew sat in the back seat between Caleb and Mary Ruth. He said to them, "I love your Bible study. My dad and mom also taught me so much. I am so sad that they were killed. I miss them so much, I don't know what is going to happen to me as I have no relatives. I was adopted when I was a little baby to very wonderful parents, thank the Lord"

Caleb said, "I know the Lord has a plan for your life."

"I'm sure He will do good for you!" replied Mary Ruth.

Len and Sandy were listening to the conversation they were having in the back seat and tears of love ran down their faces.

When they arrived at the police station, the officers put the kidnappers in a cell and then took the others in to Captain Wilson. He was shocked to see them again so soon.

Captain Wilson asked, "Weren't you here earlier?" They all sat down and told him what happened.

"The orphanage had called us and told us that someone might have kidnapped Matthew. That's why my officers happened to find you all, but they didn't know who was who"

Matthew said, "I told them who the kidnappers really were and they believed me. That was good because I'm sure that they didn't know that I never lie. I'm sure God was with us and helping us."

"You are a great boy. I've seen you in church many times and I know you talked about the Bible to other children," said Captain Wilson.

An officer then came in and gave something to Captain Wilson. Captain Wilson said, "Would you please take this young boy out with you and get him a soda and some candy? Would you like that, Matthew?"

"I am thirsty." He went out with the officer

Captain Wilson then asked the others, "What do you all have to say about Matthew?"

"He is a wonderful boy," said Mary Ruth. Then Sandy spoke and told Captain Wilson that she had a baby ten years ago in Georgia and gave him up for adoption.

"Come to think of it, Matthew does look a lot like you. We can have a DNA done and find out if he really is your son. If it is true and you want him back, I don't believe there will be any problem."

Sandy cried and said, "I do truly want him! I felt bad all my life that I gave my baby up for adoption. Thank the Lord I found him again. I have no idea who his father is. I was raped, but Len is who his father will be." She hugged Len.

"I know that everything happens for a reason. Now Matthew hopefully will be living in St. Cloud near us. I believe there is a reason also for that to happen now!" said Caleb.

"I will take a sample of blood from you so we can check your DNA compared to Matthews. I will let you know as soon as we find out. I'm pretty sure that you are his mother."

Sandy said, "I'm 100% sure! How long will it take to get the results?

"Probably a few weeks."

"Is he going to be in the orphanage till then? What if someone else tries to hurt him in some way?"

Captain Wilson replied, "We will watch him. I'll send one of my officers to stay over there to make sure that nothing happens."

"That's great! Would it be all right if I stay up here and be with him until the results come back? I haven't ever seen him, even when he was born. I would really like to be with him. He seems like a very wonderful Christian boy. I know many things happen for a reason and I believe the Lord wanted him raised by strong Christians and to learn about the Bible."

"There is a hotel about a block away from the orphanage. I will also let the orphanage know that you are permitted to visit Matthew."

"Thank you so much, Captain Wilson. I am surely looking forward to being with him. I won't tell him that I am his mother until it is proven."

Just then, Matthew came back in the room. He ran up to everyone and offered them M&M's and again said, "Thank you so very much for saving me. I love you all." He hugged and kissed them again.

Sandy asked him, "Would it be okay if I visited you for awhile?"

"I would really like that! You seem like such a nice lady."

"Great and you seem like such a nice boy!"

Captain Wilson then said, "I am going to have one of my officers take Matthew back to the orphanage and he will stay there. I thank you all for saving this boy. I don't know what would have happened if you all weren't here."

Mary Ruth said, "The Lord sent us, and we follow His will and do our best to walk in His path of rightesness."

"I do believe you all do your best to do His will and I pray that more and more people will do that also," said Captain Wilson.

Everybody kissed Matther goodbye and he left with the officer. Then they all hugged, said goodbye to Captain Wilson, and left.

When they got in the car, Sandy said to Len, "I hope what I asked to do is okay with you, but I couldn't help it. I can't wait to be with Matthew everyday!"

"I truly understand, in fact, I wish I could stay also but I have to get back to my job. I know that Captain Hardy will be so happy and shocked when I tell him this story. I'm sure he will want you to be with Matthew for awhile. Captain Hardy is a wonderful person."

Sandy kissed Len and said, "Thank you so much! I love you!"

"We are so happy for you! We will pray for you and Matthew everyday!" said Mary Ruth.

Caleb said, "Be alert to everything that seems suspicious that might hurt Matthew. I fell that, like me and Mary Ruth, Satan does not want him to meet his destiny."

"Don't worry, I'll be alert every second. Thank you, that you will be praying for us," said Sandy.

They drove down to the hotel and rented two rooms to stay overnight. Len, Caleb, and Mary Ruth will be going back to St. Cloud tomorrow and Sandy will be staying at the hotel for awhile. They got something to eat and went back to the orphanage to spend some time with Matthew.

When they were leaving, they hugged and kissed him goodbye. Matthew said, "I'm so glad you all came over to visit me before you left.

I wish you all were staying for awhile, but I'm so happy that Sandy is. Believe it or not, for some reason there is something that brings me to her." He then went up to his room.

As Sandy, Len, Caleb, and Mary Ruth got in their car, they saw that there was a police car across the street with two officers inside. They went back to the hotel and went to bed.

Sandy said to Len, "I'm going to miss you so much!"

"I'm going to miss you too! I'll call you everyday and make sure everything is all right." They went to sleep a little while later.

Chapter 7

In the morning, they left and Sandy went over to visit Matthew. He came down from his room and they sat together and talked. As they looked at each other, they both felt so much love.

"Sandy, this afternoon is the funeral for my mom and dad at the Bapist Church. They will then be buried in our Christian cemetery. Would you please come with me? I know that I'm so very sad that my parents were killed, but I do know that someday I will be with them again in Heaven. I know that they want me to be a good loving Christian person, which I definitely plan to be."

"Of course I will come with you. I will also be sad. I didn't know your parents, but I'm sure that they were great parents and great Christians who truly believed in the Lord and took great care of you. I also go to a great Bapist church in St. Cloud, Florida. I do my very best to be a good Christian and keep all the commandments."

"You are a great woman! I can feel it in my heart!"

"Are there any stores around here where I can buy some clothes? I hardly brought anything with me."

"The downtown area, where the stores are, is about a mile from here. You can call for a taxie, they're not very expensive."

"Thanks Matthew, I'll go down right now and get some clothes. What time is the funeral?"

"It's at 2PM and when it's over, we will be going to the cemetery."

"Okay, I'll be back soon." As she left the building, Sandy noticed the police officer sitting in the enterance. She thought, I'm glad a police officer is here, but I have faith that the Lord will protect Matthew.

Sandy took a cab downtown and went into a few stores for some clothes. In one of the stores, she found several things she really liked and needed. As she got in line to pay for the clothes, there were two men in front of her buying some black pants and shirts. She happened to hear what they were saying.

The one man said, "The funeral starts at 2PM, then they will be going to the cemetery. I know that Matthew will be there so when we get back to our room we have to make a good plan on how to kidnapp him again. We sure have to do better than those other two guys, who I'm sure will be put in jail for a long time."

The other man said, "That is if our boss lets them live, I know he's mad. He might kill them for not being able to accomplish what he told them to do. He's done that many times before!"

"Don't worry, we will do his orders. No one will stop us!" They had no idea that Sandy was behind them listening to their conversation.

After Sandy quickly checked out of the store, she got a taxie and went right over to the police station. She went in and asked to see Captain Wilson. The officer took her to him. Sandy introduced herself again.

Captain Wilson said, "I truly remember you! Can I help you with something?"

"You sure can!" She told him where she just was and what she heard the two men saying.

"Are you sure that's what you heard? Why would those men also want to kidnap Matthew?"

"That's exactly what they said!" She then quickly told him a few things that happened to Caleb and Mary Ruth when they were children.

"Why were all those things happening to them?

"It's a long story, but we know that Caleb and Mary Ruth have a great destiny with God. I believe it has started and is continuing more and more as they get older. When they were kids, they taught other children about our Lord, Jesus Christ. The older they get, the more they accomplish and they bring more people to the Lord! We believe that Matthew also has a destiny with the Lord. Things happen for a reason. I believe now, that is the reason I gave him up for adoption. He was adopted by a loving pastor and his wife, and learned a lot about Jesus and the Bible. Caleb and Mary Ruth do think that the people of Satan want to get rid of Matthew so he can't keep his destiny, which probably is the same as theirs."

"Don't worry, they will not get him! I'll see to that!"

Sandy was worried in her flesh about what could happen to her son, but she had complete faith in God in her spirit that He would watch over him.

When she got back to the hotel, she called Len and told him everything that happened. She said, "Please pray for Matthew!"

"Of course I will. I will always pray for him and his mother!"

Len called Caleb and Mary Ruth and told them what Sandy heard some men talking about. They all prayed to the Lord, to not allow Satan to hurt Matthew in anyway.

After Sandy prayed, she got dressed and went back to the orphanage. Matthew was ready to go. The people there gave him a nice suite to wear. He was so very sad. He hugged Sandy, as tears ran down his face.

He cried, "I'm going to miss my parents so much! I have no idea what is going to happen to me. I'm pretty sure that boys my age aren't adopted. Most people probably only want little babies, but older children need parents to love also. I know the Lord will do for me what He wants, and I'll lead a good life. I do want to be able to teach people about Jesus, like Caleb and Mary Ruth and their group do. I'm not going to be stressed out or worried. I'm going to keep my faith, and know that when the time is right, the Lord will lead me in the right direction."

Sandy hugged him again and said, "You are truly right! I do believe that you will have parents again someday and have a great life."

Matthew smiled at her and said, "Boy, that would be wonderful! How about we pray to the Lord!"

"That's a gread idea!" replied Sandy.

They held each others hands and Matthew prayed,

"OH DEAR LORD, PLEASE LEAD ME AND GUIDE ME TO WALK IN YOUR NARROW PATH OF RIGHTIONESS AND DO YOUR WILL. I KNOW THAT I AM ONLY A YOUNG BOY, BUT I GIVE MYSELF TO YOU. YOU ARE MY EVERYTHING AND ALWAYS WILL BE. PLEASE HAVE ME KEEP YOUR COMMANDMENTS. I WANT TO LOVE EVERYONE, BE KIND TO THEM, BRING MORE AND MORE PEOPLE TO REPENT OF THEIR SINS, BELIEVE IN OUR LORD AND SAVIOR, JESUS CHRIST, AND WHAT HE DID FOR US ON THE CROSS. IT WAS WONDERFUL THAT HE LOVED US

SO MUCH. I THANK YOU THAT I HAD MY WONDERFUL PARENTS, AS LONG AS I DID. I TRULY BELIEVE THAT THINGS WILL WORK OUT FOR ME. I LOVE, TRUST, AND HAVE FAITH IN YOU. IN JESUS HOLY NAME, AMEN."

"That was a great prayer! We better get going," cried Sandy.

A woman, named Debbie, who worked at the orphanage, was a member of the Baptist Church and went with them to the funeral. She took them in her car.

When they arrived at the Baptist Church, Matthew's parents were in their open coffins. Matthew held both their hands, prayed, and knew their spirits were now with the Lord.

The funeral was very nice and many people went up and talked about his parents. Matthew also went up and said very wonderful things about them. When it was over, they got in the car with Debbie and she headed for the cemetery. Debbie had to go back to her job and asked them if they had a way back to the orphanage.

Sandy said, "Don't worry, we can take a taxi back. Thank you for bringing us. See you later. Bye." They all hugged each other and Debbie left.

As Sandy and Matthew were walking up to the burial place, she was wondering why she didn't see any police cars or officers when they arrived.

There were many people getting out of their cars. After the burial was over, Sandy thought, I'm so glad nothing happened! Were those guys talking about something else?

As they were walking to the street to get a taxi, two men dressed in black walked up to them. The one man said, "Matthew, we're so sorry about what you've been through. We're going to help you get out of your problems."

Sandy and Matthew just looked at each other. The other man brought out a gun and told Sandy to let go of Matthew's hand, that he would be going with them.

Sandy squeezed Matthew's hand, then jumped in front of him. She said, "You will never take this child from me!"

The one man looked at her and said "Goodbye," as the other man was ready to shoot her.

Sandy then heard a shot, but didn't feel anything. Suddenly, the man with the gun fell down on the ground. The other man started running. Next thing, three men ran after him and caught him. Two others ran up to the man on the ground and grabbed the gun.

One of the men said to Sandy, "We're police officers! Captain Wilson had us dress as others, so the criminals didn't know who we are. It worked out, thankfully, Matthew was not kidnapped again. From now on, an officer will be staying at the orphanage with him, twenty four hours a day to protect him. Sandy and Matthew hugged each other and Matthew said, "Sandy, I love you and thank you for trying to save me."

Sandy said to the officers, "Thank you so much for saving my life also." She shook hands with all of them.

Chapter 8

An officer took Sandy and Matthew back to the orphanage. Sandy stayed with Matthew for awhile. As they talked, Sandy felt they were becoming closer and closer together. They thanked the Lord again for saving Matthew. Sandy remembered all the things Caleb and Mary Ruth had been through.

As she was going back to her hotel, she sat down and prayed that Matthew would continue to be safe. When she reached her hotel room, she called Len and told him what happened.

He was stunned! He said, "I am sure he has a destiny with the Lord!"

"I believe that also. Thank you for praying for Matthew."

"Caleb, Mary Ruth, and their group also prayed for him. I'll call them again and tell them what happened. I know they will continue to pray for him and I believe that the Lord will be with Matthew. I love you and miss you so much!"

"Hopfully, it won't be to long until I find out if I'm truly Matthew's mother."

Len said, "Captain Hardy was so shocked to hear what happened, but he was so happy to hear that Matthew might be your son. He said to tell you that he misses you and not to worry about your job. It will be here for you whenever you return."

Two weeks went by. Sandy and Matthew did get closer and closer. One morning as Sandy was ready to go over to see Matthew, someone knocked on her door. She looked through the peep hole and saw a police officer. She opened the door.

The officer said, "Hi, Captain Wilson sent me here to bring you over to him. He said to tell you that he has finally gotten the report of the DNA back."

Sandy cried, "What did it say!"

"He didn't tell me. He only told me to come over and get you."

Sandy cried again, "Let's go!"

They got in the car and left. Sandy was so excited. When they arrived at the police station, she went into Captain Wilson's office, shook hands with him and sat down.

Captain Wilson said, "You know what the wonderful news is! You are definitely Matthew's mother!"

Sandy jumped up, thanked and praised the Lord with all her heart, that she was able to have her son.

She hugged Captain Wilson and cried because she was so very happy that she is Matthew's mother.

"I do believe you have a wonderful son and I'm so glad you got him back!"

"Am I going to be able to have him forever?"

"I will get in touch with the orphanage, they will get in touch with the state and tell them about you. They probably will check what they can about your life and interview you to make sure you will be a great mother. It will take a little more time, but I'm sure that it will work out."

"Thank you so much, I can't wait to be with Matthew and tell him that I am his mother."

"I wish you all good luck! I know that you'll have a wonderful life together."

"Thank you so much!" cried Sandy.

An officer took her to the orphanage. Matthew was sitting on the couch waiting for her. Sandy ran up to him and hugged him strongly.

Matthew said, "I was wondering why you weren't here yet and praying that nothing happened to you."

"Thank you for praying for me, but something wonderful has happened to me!"

"What could have happened this morning that is so wonderful?"

"I have something to tell you, but I had to wait until I found out that it was really true."

"Please tell me!" said Matthew.

"I am your real mother!" cried Sandy.

Matthew just looked at her in shock! He said, "If you are my mother, why did you give me up when I was a baby?"

She explained to him what happened to her and told him how very sorry she was that she did give him up.

She was surprised when Matther said, "I believe that it happened for a reason. God wanted me to be raised by very Christian people and I was. I learned so much through them. Now He is giving me back to you. I feel that there is something that you are going to do for my life."

"Truly there is! First of all, you will have a loving mother and father, who truly believes in the Lord. Also, you can be with Caleb and Mary Ruth and learn more about the Bible. I believe that you have a very great destiny as I know they do."

Matthew and Sandy hugged and kissed each other. They then thanked the Lord with all their heart and soul. Sandy stayed and they talked for awhile about all kind of things, then she ran back to her hotel room to call Len.

Back at St. Cloud, Len just got home from work when the phone rang. He picked up the phone and said, "Hello." It was Jane, his mother in law. She said, "Hi, are you and Sandy okay? I haven't heard from either one of you in over two weeks. Is something wrong? I called a few times and there was either no answer or the line was busy. Is Sandy there?"

Len didn't know what to tell her about all the things that happened. He knew Sandy would want to. He also knew that Jane and Josh would be completely shocked when they met their grandson and heard the entire story.

He said, "No, Sandy isn't here right now. She's been really busy for the past few weeks. "We're doing lots of things to help our lives."

"That's great, but I do like to talk to my daughter sometimes. Could you please have her call me? Josh and I miss not being with her, you to Len!"

"We miss you and Josh to, we love you both. I'll tell her to call you."

"Thank you Len, bye, bye."

Just as he hung up the phone, it started ringing again. It was Sandy. Len told her about her mom just being on the phone with him.

Sandy said, "I'm so sorry, I should have remembered to call her, but I kind of was in another world, meeting Matthew and spending time with him. Guess what Len! I found out today that Matthew is truly my son."

"I felt that was really true. As many people even said how much he looked like you. I already love him and can't wait to be his dad!"

Thank you so much Len! It means so much to me! I'll call my mom from here, but I'm not going to tell her anything about what happened until I return with Matthew and I can take him over to their home and tell them everything. It won't be much longer. My life has to be checked and I have to be interviewed to make sure that I will be a good mother."

"I agree that is a good way to do it. I won't say anything about what happened, and I'll also tell Caleb and Mary Ruth not to say anything either. They will be so happy to hear that you are Matthew's mother. I love you! See you soon. Bye."

Sandy called her parent's home. Her mom answered the phone. Sandy said, "Hi mom, I'm sorry I haven't seen or talked to you or dad for awhile, but I am really busy."

Jane asked, "How could you be so busy that you couldn't even call us?"

"It's a long story and I know that you and dad will understand when I come over and talk to you. I pray that you will forgive me."

"Forgive you? What did you do for me to have to forgive you?"

"As I said, it's a long story."

"I hope you and Len didn't break up!"

"No mom, Len and I love each other more than ever. You will understand. It will be a few days until I can come over because I'm still doing things. I have to go now. See you and dad soon. I love you!"

"We love you too, honey. Bye bye"

Jane went and told Josh what just happened on the phone. Josh said, "I wonder what is going on with her? I can't imagine!"

"Neither can I! I'm going to call her back. I know she's at work but I will only talk to her for a few minutes."

Jane called the police department where Sandy worked. A male officer answered the phone. Jane asked, "Can I please speak to Sandy?"

The officer said, "I'm sorry, she isn't here."

"Where is she?"

"As far as I know, she's up in Georgia for about the last two or three weeks."

44

"She's in Georgia? What is she doing there?"

He said, "I'm sorry, I have no idea."

"Well, thank you. Bye."

She ran over and told Josh what now happened. Josh said, "Maybe she's visiting her sister, Judy. Actually, we should be visiting her too. We have not seen them for awhile. I wish they lived closer. I always think about our grandaughter, Esther."

"I've talked to Judy on the phone several times and she never said anything about Sandy being there. I'm going to call her right now and find out if Sandy is there." Jane called, Judy answered the phone and said, "Hello."

Jane yelled, "Judy, is Sandy there? I just heard that she has been in Georgia now for two or three weeks! Is she with you?"

"Calm down, mom! No, she isn't here. I haven't seen or heard from her for at least a month. I have no idea where she is or what she's doing. I'm sure she is doing all right. You know that she is a very faithful, loving, Christian person."

"Yes, I surely know that, but why didn't she let me know what's going on."

"I'm sure there is a reason why she didn't tell you."

"She did say she would see me in a few days and tell me and your dad all about what has been happening."

"See mom, don't worry, have faith that she is going to tell you something good."

"You're right, Judy, thanks for helping me do what is right and have faith in God. Please give my grandaughter a big hug and a kiss from her grandparents. Tell her that we love her and miss her and can't wait to see her again. Also tell your husband we love him. I love you too, so very much!"

"Bye mom, please let me know what happened."

"I sure will! Bye , bye."

Again, Jane told Josh what happened when she talked to Judy. Josh said, "Judy told you the very right thing to do. Don't be upset. We will soon see Sandy and she will tell us what happened. Be calm."

Jane went to the kitchen and made lunch. She kept thinking, What could be going on? I need to find out ASAP. I'm sorry that I worry. I love Sandy so much, she has been through many things, but the Lord was always with her and saved her. I'm going to stop worrying right now and have faith that Sandy is going to tell us something good!

A couple days later, a state officer came to the orphanage, talked with Sandy, and then told her that they decided that she could have Matthew. He had Sandy read and sign some papers, plus give him a lot of information.

He said to Sandy and Matthew, "I wish you a wonderful life together." Sandy and Matthew thanked him and hugged each other. Sandy said, "Tomorrow and the next day, Len is on his day offs, boy, that works out really good for us. You will be staying with me tonight at the hotel. I'll call Len and tell him the great news!"

Sandy called Len that evening when he got home from work and told him the news. She also told him about all the papers she had to sign and all the information she had to give the state.

"I wish we had a little bit bigger home since we have a son now. We used just about all of our savings to pay for the hotel and all the phone calls we made," replied Len.

"Don't worry, I'm sure we will be very happy where we live. Would you like to talk to Matthew? He'll be staying here with me tonight."

"I can't wait to see him again! Please put him on the phone."

Matthew got on the phone and said, "Hello Len, can I call you dad?"

"You sure can! I can't wait to be with you and be your dad! I know that you're a wonderful boy! I mean, wonderful son!"

"I know I will again have wonderful parents. I truly thank God for what he has now done for me."

"I truly thank God too! He has been so good to me and Sandy. I will see you tomorrow afternoon. I love you. Bye."

Matthew hung up the phone and said to Sandy, "Mom. I can't wait to go to St. Cloud and have parents again. I am still very sad about what happened to my adopted parents, but the Lord has lead me in his path of righteousness, where I always want to be." Again, they hugged and kissed each other.

Matthew asked, "Can we go over to my parents home and get my clothes and other things I have, can we take them to St. Cloud?"

"Sure, I never even thought about that!"

Len left St. Cloud very early the next morning and got to the hotel around 11 AM. He knocked on the door of Sandy's room. Sandy and Matthew both opened it and they all hugged and kissed each other. The first thing they did was get down on their knees and thanked the Lord for all he did for them.

Len said, "Let me take you to lunch, then we can head to St. Cloud."

"We're ready for lunch, but after lunch, we have to go where Matthew used to live to get some of his things to take with us," replied Sandy.

"How are we going to get in?" asked Len.

Matthew said, "I have a key."

"Okay, that's what we'll do."

After lunch, Matthew told Len the address and how to get there. They pulled up in front of the house, it was very nice. Matthew opened the door and they went in. The inside was beautiful.

Sandy said, "Oh boy, you lived in a really great house. I'm sorry that the one your going to move into is way smaller than this."

"It doesn't matter to me where I live, as long as I'm with great people that believe in the Lord like I do. I know I am still a young child, but I always thank the Lord for helping me. I always put him first in my life."

"That's so wonderful, we are so glad that we have you. God led us to come here and do what we did," replied Len.

They went in the basement and Matthew found a big suit case. They went to his room and packed clothes and everything else he wanted, including his Bible.

Before they left, Matthew went into his parent's bedroom and again, tears came from his eyes.

Sandy hugged him and said, "I know you miss your parents, but I also believe that the parents you have now will be very good to you."

Matthew kissed her and said, "I truly believe that the Lord has brought us together." They locked the house up, got in the car, and headed for St. Cloud.

Chapter 9

That evening they got to their home. The first thing they did was show Matthew around the house and took his suit case into his bedroom. Len and Matthew sat down and talked about St Cloud, while Sandy called her parents. Her mom always answered the phone. Sandy said, "Hi mom!"

Jane asked, "Sandy, where are you?"

"I'm at my house, mom."

"I heard you were in Georgia for quite awhile. I called your sister to see if that was where you were, but she said she haden't seen you or heard from you for a month! What in the world is going on? How could you leave your job and be somewhere in Georgia by yourself?"

"Mom, it's a long, wonderful, exciting story! We will come over tomorrow morning and tell you and dad everything! You both will be surprised, shocked, and I pray, very happy!"

"This sounds very interesting. Why would we feel all those things you just said?"

"You and dad will understand tomorrow and I pray your not mad at me."

"What could possibly make us mad at you? You're a wonderful daughter and I know someday you will give us wonderful grandchildren to love."

Sandy was surprised when her mom said that. "We will be over in the morning. I love you and dad so much!"

"We love you too, Sandy, and always will. Bye, I am looking forward to seeing you and Len tomarrow."

Len had ordered a delicious pizza from Riccio's. They sat down, ate it, and talked for awhile. Matthew told them some of the things that happened in his life and how the Lord always healed him and taught him things. The Lord also gave him the wisdom and understanding of the Bible.

Sandy said, "Many things also happened to us, mainly concerning Caleb and Mary Ruth. The Lord took care of us in so many ways."

She looked at Len and he said, "How very true. We also can tell you many stories some day. Well, it's getting late. We'll help you unpack your suit case, then we'll all go to bed. You know that tomorrow morning you'll be meeting your grandparents."

"I'm sorry to say this, but they never knew that I had a baby, so when we go there, they will have no idea that you are their grandson. I will tell them the whole story of what happened. I'm sure they will love you forever!" said Sandy.

Matthew asked, "Who is my real father? Is it Len?"

"No, unfortunately not. Just listen while I talk to my parents, you will also hear what happened to me."

"I sure will listen! I would really like to meet my real father."

Sandy felt sad when Matthew said that. "Okay, we'll get up tomorrow, have some breakfast, and go right over to my parents. They only live a few blocks from here."

After they helped Matthew unpack and hang his clothes up, they all went to bed. They got up early. After breakfast, they drove over to Jane and Josh's home. Sandy knocked on the door and they both answered. They hugged and kissed Sandy and Len, then noticed the little boy.

Josh said, "We haven't seen you for quite awhile! What a cute little boy you have with you. Who is he?"

"His name is Matthew. He's going to be living with us," replied Sandy.

Jane smiled and said, "How nice!" She and Josh hugged him and said, "It's so niice to meet you!"

Matthew smiled and said, "It is so nice to meet you too!" He was so happy that he met his grandparents, but he didn't say anything else. They went into the living room and sat down.

Sandy started telling them about when she was out for a walk one evening and hurt her foot. Her mom said, "I remember that."

Sandy then told them about the man who insisted on driving her home and what happened after she got in the car. Jane and Josh were shocked to hear this and so was Matthew. She told them how she became pregnant, stayed at her sister's in Georgia and gave the baby up for adoption.

Josh asked, "Do you mean Judy knew what happened and never told us?"

"I made her and her husband promise me and God that they would never tell anyone what happened. They kept their promise."

Sandy then told them why she never got pregnant after she married Len. She was taking pills because she felt she had to for giving up her son, but Len did find out what she was doing and she told him the whole story. He forgave her and she did stop taking the pills, but never got pregnant.

Len replied, "Then I went to be checked and was told that I had a very low sperm count. We might never have children."

Jane said, "Oh no! We do have your sister's wonderful daughter, but we were hoping that you would have children too."

All of a sudden, Josh said, "I remember, that happened about ten years ago." All of a sudden, Jane and Josh both looked at Matthew and realized that he looked a lot like Sandy!

Sandy cried, "This is your grandson!!!!!!!!!!!"

Jane and Josh were in shock, but they ran over to Matthew, hugged and kissed him. They all were crying tears of love and happiness! Jane and Josh put Matthew in between them on the couch and couldn't stop hugging and kissing him!

Jane cried, "Oh Sandy, thank you for our beautiful grandson!!!!!!"

Josh cried, "How did you find him and are now able to keep him?"

Sandy and Len told her parents what happened in the last month. Jane and Josh were shocked again to hear this story. Jane hugged Matthew and said, "Thank God Matthew was saved! Some of these things sound like what had happened to Caleb and Mary Ruth."

Sandy then explained to them who Matthew's adopted parents were, what happened to them, and how Matthew knows so much already about being a good Christian through them.

Josh hugged Matthew and said, "We're so very sorry your adopted parents were killed. This is a very wonderful thing that's happening to us. We now have a wonderful grandson and will be with him now and for the rest of our lives!"

"Sandy, we're not mad at you for what you did. Like you say, many things happen for a reason. I believe you did what the Lord wanted you to do."

Mathew then said, "I had a very good life with my adopted parents, and I truly miss them, but I truly feel that I will continue to have a great life and do God's will. I would like to say a prayer now." They all held hands and closed their eyes.

"THANK YOU, DEAR LORD, FOR BEING WITH ME, HELPING ME, LEADING ME, AND GUIDING ME. I AM SO VERY THANKFUL THAT I AM HERE WITH MY REAL MOTHER AND A WONDERFUL STEP FATHER. THANK YOU SO MUCH FOR GIVING ME LOVING GRANDPARENTS ALSO. I KNOW YOU WILL CONTINUE TO BE WITH ME AND HELP ME TO MEET MY TRUE DESTINY. I GIVE MYSELF TO YOU, WANT TO DO YOUR WILL, AND WALK IN YOUR NARROW PATH OF RIGHTEOUSNESS ALWAYS. I LOVE YOU, TRUST YOU, AND HAVE FAITH IN YOUR WILL, WITH ALL MY HEART AND SOUL. THANK YOU FOR YOUR HOLY SPIRIT THAT IS IN ME, THROUGH YOUR SON, OUR LORD AND SAVIOR, JESUS CHRIST. AMEN."

Again, they all hugged each other and were so happy! Sandy said, "We have to put Matthew in school, just like we did with Caleb and Mary Ruth."

"I also know that you have to go back to work, Sandy. I will be more than glad to take care of him," said Jane.

"Me too!" cried Josh.

"Thank you mom and dad. I love you so much! You are such wonderful parents! You have helped me and others so much."

Jane then said to Matthew, "Let's all get going to church and after, you all can come back here for lunch, okay?

"I'm looking forward to going to your Baptist Church and having lunch with my grandparents after church," said Matthew.

They went to church and many people noticed Matthew and wondered who he was. Jane knew that they were wondering about Matthew, she could see everyone looking at him.

After church, she said to her friends, "Meet our grandson, Matthew." They all shook hands with him, smiled, and said, "Glad to meet you."

Jane said, "I know your wondering how I got a grandson all of a sudden. It's a long story, but a very interesting one. Now we have to be with and get to know our wonderful grandson." They went back to Jane and Josh's home and had lunch.

Matther thanked the Lord that he was now with Sandy, Len, Jane and Josh. They all thanked the Lord for Matthew.

"We're going to go down now and visit Caleb, Mary Ruth, and their grandparents, that they live with," announced Len.

"I would really like that," replied Matthew. "I can't wait to see Caleb and Mary Ruth again!"

They drove down to their home at the lake. Luckily, they were all there. They knocked on the door. Thelma opened it and was so happy to see them. She brought them into the living room where Tom, Caleb, and Mary Ruth were.

When Caleb and Mary Ruth saw them, they were so excited to see that Matthew was with them. They hugged and kissed everyone.

Mary Ruth said to Matthew, " We're so very glad that you are here!"

"So am I," cried Matthew. "I'm sure it is the will of God."

They all held hands and Caleb prayed and thanked God for all He had done for Matthew and for bringing him here.

Tom said, "What a great young boy you have! When Caleb and Mary Ruth came home from Georgia, they told us what happened. Thelma and I prayed for Matthew and of course Caleb, Mary Ruth, and their wonderful group did also.

Thelma asked, "How did you and Len ever get to bring Matthew here?"

Sandy then explained that she was his real mother and it was proven with a DNA testing from each of them, then she explained the entire story of what happened after Len, Caleb, and Mary Ruth went home.

Thelma cried, ""Matthew, I know you have true faith in the Lord, like Caleb and Mary Ruth do! I feel it."

Tom then said, "Oh boy, Thelma, this means that Jane and Josh now have a grandson. How wonderful! I'm sure that they all know that Matthew has a destiny with God."

Matthew replied, "I always felt that way. I do have a destiny with the Lord!"

"We will be more than glad to teach you and have you with us, and our group. Their names are, Tammy, Pepi, Michael, and Raymond," said Caleb.

"Thank you so much. I can't wait to be with you all. I used to listen to you every morning on the radio at my home, but when I was put in the orphanage, I had no radio to listen to. Unfortunatlly, I missed your teaching for awhile." Matthew said.

"I'll be glad to tell you about all the teachings you missed." replied Mary Ruth.

"Tomorrow we have to get Matthew put into school, but everyday after school, if it's okay, he can come over to your house and I can pick him up around 5 PM when I finish my job."

"That would be great!"

"It sure would, then if we go to my grandparents home, I can help my grandma make supper!"

"You mean you know how to make supper?" asked Sandy.

"Yes, I'm pretty good, my step mother used to have me help her all the time. I liked it and so did she. She taught me a lot about cooking."

Len said, "Wow, I'm sure it's good to know how to cook. Sandy and your grandma can teach you even more. They both are great cooks."

After they talked for awhile, Sandy said, "It was so nice spending time with you all. Now we will have to go home and Matthew and I will make supper." They all hugged each other and said, "We'll see you all again soon."

They went back to their house. Sandy and Len were very impressed as Matthew helped Sandy make the meal. The meal was delicious!

Len hugged Matthew and said, "Thank you so much for helping Sandy! You did a wonderful job!"

"I will be going back to work tomorrow, your mom will be taking you to the school so you can start here in August."

You'll be in 5th grade, right?" asked Sandy.

"Actually, I'll be in 6th grade this year," replied Matthew.

"That means that you will be going to our junior high school. That's where we'll go tomorrow." They all sat down and talked a lot about each other's life. They were all amazed. They truly loved each other and truly loved the Lord.

Sandy said, "I am so glad that Caleb and Mary Ruth came into our lives. Things happened for a reason and at the proper time everything worked out, thanks to the Lord. He is so wonderful when you believe, have faith and complete trust in Him. I know that Caleb, Mary Ruth and their group are having so many people understand that and I fell that someday you will be in their group, Matthew."

"That is truly what I would love to do!" cried Matthew.

Chapter 10

Next day, Len went to work and Sandy took Matthew to the St. Cloud Jr. High School. All the teachers were there preparing for the coming year. They met the principal, talked with him and gave him the name of the school Matthew used to attend, so they could get his records.

On the way home, they stopped at Sandy's parent's home and visited them for awhile. Sandy told them that Matthew would be going to school in two weeks and she would be going back to work tomorrow.

Jane asked, "Does that mean that Matthew will be staying with us while your working?"

"It sure does, if you and dad don't mind."

"You know we're looking forward to it," cried Jane, as she hugged Matthew.

Josh said, "If you want us to, we can take you different places around here. There's a beautiful place in Winter Haven called, Cypress Gardens. We would love to take you there. It's so nice, plus there are many other places we can take you. We'll have a good time together!"

"I'll be so glad to be with my grandparents! I'll go anywhere with you, but I also would like to go down and be with Caleb and Mary Ruth."

Jane said, "No problem. I'm sure that is one of the best places you can be!"

"I will bring him over around 7:45 in the morning and pick him up around 5:15 in the afternoon."

"We're looking forward to being with Matthew," said her dad.

"Okay, see you tomorrow morning." Sandy took Matthew over to Riccio's for lunch and they each had a great sub. They went back home and started putting the rest of his things away in his tiny bedroom.

"I'm so sorry that this house isn't like your other home. When we bought this, we thought we could eventually buy a bigger one when we started having kids, but we never had any. Now we have a wonderful son, but not very much money to buy a bigger home, even if we sell this one."

"I love you both so much. Please don't worry about this house. It's fine with me and I'm so grateful to God that he sent me here."

Matthew had a wonderful two weeks with his grandparents. He also was with Caleb and Mary Ruth a lot. It was so tremendous, learning more and more of the Bible. Sandy and Len also got him a radio for his bedroom, so he could listen to the teachings every morning as he was getting ready for school.

In November, Sandy was feeling strange one day. She thought, What is going on in me? I feel so different. She kept feeling that way for several days, then started throwing up and told Len about it.

"I want you to go to your doctor and be checked out." Matthew also heard what she said. "We will pray for you that everything will be fine."

Sandy made an appointment and went to her doctor's. He examined her whole body and took her blood.

Dr. Byron said, "Come back next week and we should know what's causing your problems and we'll help you. Be careful, don't smoke or drink any liquor."

"Don't worry about that. I never smoked a cigarette or drank any liquor in my life. I know those things are not good for your health."

She was sick that whole week. Finally, she went back to the doctors. She sat down in the room and waited for him. When Dr. Byron came in, he had a big smile on his face. He shook her hand and she wondered why he was smiling at her.

"Believe it or not, you are about a month and a half pregnant!"

"What? I thought I couldn't get pregnant because of Len's problem!"

"Yes, that is true, but I did tell Len that there was a very slight chance for you to get pregnant some day. Apparently, this is the time."

Sandy was so thrilled! She hugged the doctor and cried in happiness. The doctor then said, "Your baby is due around June 15. I will give you some medicine to help you with your baby and something else to help you with your nausea."

"I can't wait to tell Len, Matthew, my parents and everyone I know about this. They'll be so happy! We all were so happy and thankful that Matthew came into our lives, now another child, how wonderful!"

Sandy left and got back in her car, she thanked the Lord with all her heart and soul. She got back to work and took her pills. Awhile later, she started feeling better.

Len arrived back at the police station around 4:30. Sandy saw him enter, ran up to him, and said, "Len, I have to talk to you right now! Let's go out on the porch."

Len thought, I know Sandy was at the doctors today, I pray to God that it isn't bad news! They sat down on the bench.

Sandy held Len's hands and said, "I have something to tell you and I know that you'll be shocked."

Again, Len said in his mind, "Oh please Lord, I pray she is okay!"

Sandy shouted, "Len, we're going to have a baby!"

Len nearly fainted. "What? Are you sure?"

"Of course I'm sure! The baby is due around June 15."

Len cried, "The doctor did tell me that there was a slight chance that this could happen, but I guess I never believed it."

They hugged and kissed each other. They were so happy! They looked up and thanked the Lord. They then went to pick Matthew up at Sandy's parent's home.

As they were driving, Len said, "Wow, your parents and Matthew are really going to be surprised!"

They got to the house and went inside. Sandy told them all that she was pregnant and due in June. Matthew cried, "I would love to have a little brother or sister! I can't wait!"

Jane and Josh were so happy when they heard the news. Jane said, "A few monthes ago we only had one wonderful grandaughter, Esther, living in Georgia. Then we got our wonderful grandson, Matthew. Now in about seven months. We will have another one! The Lord is so wonderful to us, and we are so very thankful to Him."

Len said, "He also is so very good to us. Let's all thank Him!"

They all got down on their knees and Len prayed,

"DEAR LORD, WE TRULY THANK YOU FOR ALL THE WONDERFUL THINGS YOU HAVE DONE FOR US, HOW YOU HEALED US, HOW YOU SAVED OUR LIVES. WE ARE SO

VERY GRATEFUL TO YOU. I NEVER EXPECTED TO HAVE SANDY BECOME PREGNANT, BUT THANKS TO YOU, SHE IS, AND WE ARE SO LOOKING FORWARD TO HAVING OUR BABY! I AM SO GLAD THAT WE TRULY BELIEVE IN YOU AND HAVE FAITH, TRUST, AND HOPE ALWAYS. I ALSO PRAY THAT OTHERS WILL UNDERSTAND AND TRULY LOVE YOU AS WE DO. THANK YOU WITH ALL OUT HEARTS, SOULS, AND MINDS. IN JESUS HOLY NAME, AMEN."

They all hugged and kissed each other. Matthew said to Len, "I really loved your prayer. What you said is so true and my goal in life is to have Christians understand that there is more to do than just going to church. We need to bring people to Jesus and teach them to read and understand the Bible and follow it. I'm so very glad that Caleb, Mary Ruth, and their group are doing the Bible study on the radio, so more and more people can understand. They are also answering questions that people send to them. I will be seeing them tomorrow. I'll tell them the great news, that you are having a baby. I guess we're going home now to have supper."

As they were driving home, Sandy said, "I wish our house was a little bigger."

"Don't worry about that, just be thankful that we're having a baby," replied Len.

Everything was going fine. One morning, they got a phone call. It was a man from Atlanta, Georgia, named Luke Harney. Sandy was just about ready to leave to take Matthew to school, then go to work.

Luke said, "I have heard that you are Matthew's real mother and now he is living with you."

"That's certainly true. He is such a wonderful son."

"I was wondering if Matthew was going to sell his other parents house in Atlanta."

"What? You mean that now it belongs to Matthew? We never knew that or thought about it, we were just so thankful that we had Matthew."

"I'm sure his step parents had a will. You need to check into it. If Matthew wants to sell the house, please let me know the price, because I love it. It's really nice. My phone number is 525-521-4320."

"I'll call you back, ASAP, as soon as I find out what's going on."

"Thank you, bye."

Matthew was in the car waiting for Sandy. She got in and asked Matthew, "Did you know that you now might own your adopted parent's home?"

"No I didn't, I never thought that it would belong to me. Just think, there's a lot of beautiful things inside, including some of mine. I had no idea what would happen to that house."

"When I have time at work, I'm going to call the state of Georgia and ask them to tell me what is going on."

"That's a good idea," said Matthew.

Sandy drove to the school, gave Matthew a kiss and said, "Have a good day. I'll see you later and let you know what happened."

During her lunch hour, Sandy called Georiga. She introduced herself and talked with a very nice man and asked him why Matthew Jones, her real son, now Matthew Gordon, didn't know any thing about his parents having a will."

"I'm sure it was because the will had to go through probate, and it does take awhile. Let me call you back after I check things out. It might take awhile."

Sandy gave him her phone number at her job and they said goodbye. At 4:30, Sandy still did not heard from Georgia. At 4:45 her phone rang and it was the man she had been speaking to earlier.

The man said, "I'm sorry it has taken me so long to call you back. At first, I couldn't locate anything. It took awhile, which is really unusual. It seems like some man that we never even heard of wrote that he had notified you of your son's adopted parent's will. We couldn't believe that happened and are so sorry. Give me your address and I'll send you everything."

"Thank you so much!" Sandy gave him their address and thanked him again.

She picked Matthew up at Caleb and Mary Ruth's home. When he got in the car, she told him what happened.

Matthew said, "Isn't it strange that a man wrote that he sent us everything and they probably didn't even look at his name at that time."

"Yes, it is weird."

"Do you think that it could have been one of the evil men? Maybe for some reason they don't want me to have anything."

"You might be right!" said Sandy.

"I can't wait to get the letter. I'm sure my adopted parents left me something. I know how much they loved me and I loved them. What will be, will be."

"I am so glad that we love the Lord so much and have faith in Him. It is amazing how HE has been with us and helped us in all situations. He has received us and taken care of us always."

"I wish more people would realize how wonderful it is to believe in and have complete faith in God. They also must keep the commandments and do their best to be a good loving person to others. People who do not study the Bible do not know or understand why things happen. I heard a lot of them ask my adopted father, "Why isn't God helping us? Why are all these bad things happening?" Most people don't even know that Satan is over the earth and he can lead you to do wrong things. He can cause a lot of trouble, without them even knowing it was Satan who deceived them into doing evil things."

"You're absolutely right! Satan causes lots of trouble but if we have complete faith in the Lord, He will take care of us. Many people don't have complete faith. If everyone in this world learned from the Bible, understood and obeyed, this would be a very different world," replied Sandy.

"Yes, and when our Lord and Savior returns to us, things will be different. We don't know when that will be, even Jesus doesn't know. God, His father, will tell Him when to return. That's another reason I'm glad that I came back to my real mother. I'm also hoping that someday I can be with Caleb and Mary Ruth in their ministry. They are such great Christians!"

"I do feel that being with them is part of your destiny," said Sandy.

Chapter 11

A few days later, they received the letter from Georgia, with the copy of Matthew's adopted parents will. Len, Sandy, and Matthew sat down on the couch and Sandy started reading it to them. It mainly said that Matthew's adopted parents were giving everything to their wonderful son, Matthew, including the house, everything in it, whatever money they had in the bank, their car, and all their wonderful Bible material.

Matthew again had tears running down his face. He said, "How great of my wonderful step parents to leave everything to me. What will I do with everything?"

Sandy said, "You know that there is a man wanting to buy the house. That's how we got started in this whole thing. If Len can change his days off with another officer and be off on a weekend, we can drive up there and check out everything in the house. Maybe Paul will allow us to borrow his truck, then we can bring what you want back here for you. I'm sorry we don't have much room in this house. Do you want to sell the car?"

"No, we can hopefully bring it down here," said Matthew.

Len said, "Sure, Sandy and you can ride back in the car and I'll drive the truck. If you want, we'll ask the man who wants to buy the house how much he wants to offer before we put it up for sale."

"I can call him and let him know when we're coming up and he can meet us at the house. We can show him the inside."

"Okay, let me find out what weekend I can get off and I'm sure Paul will lend me his truck."

"Great, I'm looking forward to it," replied Matthew.

During the week, Len traded his days off with one of his friends and talked to Paul about borrowing his truck and told him what was going on.

Paul said, "No problem. When are you going up to Georgia?"

"Two weeks from now."

Paul said, "Believe it or not, I'm also off that weekend. Would you like me to come and help you?"

"Thank you so much! That would be really great."

When Len got home after work that day, he told Sandy and Matthew when they would be going, that Paul is lending us his truck, and he offered to come with us and help!

"That's great! Paul is such a wonderful man. Matthew, you don't know him yet, but he is a great friend of ours. He was stranded on the island with us. It's really a strange story of how we met him. He helped us so much, and he is also a faithful, loving, Christian person. He knows a lot about the Bible and was with Caleb and Mary Ruth a lot. At that time, on the island, Caleb was your age and Mary Ruth was only seven. You will be surprised to hear many more of our stories and how God always helped and took care of us."

Matthew said, "I'm sure they are amazing stories! I assume that Satan was trying to stop Caleb and Mary Ruth from their future destiny, but thanks to the Lord, it never happened."

"You're completely right! Things even happened to your grandparents, but thank the Lord, they survived. In fact, let's invite them over to dinner on Sunday, and you and I can make it."

"That would be great! I love being with them. I know you and I can make a great meal together."

Sandy called her parents and invited them. Jane said, "That sounds wonderful. We can't wait to be with Matthew again. He is so sweet! I wish your sister could come down so he can meet his Aunt Judy, Uncle John, and especially his cousin, Esther. I'm sure they will love each other."

"Would you like me to call and invite them down this weekend?"

"That would be wonderful, I hope they will be able to come. I know that they do a lot of great things on the weekend to help poor people. I'm sure that they want to meet Matthew."

"I'll call her right now! Bye, bye."

Sandy called Judy and asked her to please come down and meet Matthew and told her that she also has a surprise to tell them.

"Don't worry, we will be there, in fact, we will leave early Saturday morning We didn't have anything to do this weekend, but we have a great thing to do now!. We will be able to go to church with you all on Sunday. Can we stay at your house?"

"Judy, I'm so sorry, but it would be better for you to stay at mom and dads, only because we have very little room and right now we can't afford to buy a bigger house."

"I wish I could help you, but we use a lot of our money to help the poor and needy people. I'm not going to have any more children, so our home is fine. Thank the Lord that I do have a wonderful daughter, who we love so much. We can't wait to meet Matthew. I truly remember when you gave birth to him. I was with you and you were so sad. It is truly a miracle that you got him back!"

"Yes it is! I'm so very thankful to the Lord! We can't wait to see you all on Saturday. You won't believe this, but Matthew is a great cook!"

"That's interesting, because Esther is a great cook too! I've been teaching her since she was a little child."

"If she wants to work with Matthew, that would be fine. I probably won't have much to do with both of them."

Judy laughed, "I'm sure it will be great! See you soon! Bye."

Sandy told Matthew and Len that Judy, John, and Esther would be here on Saturday and how Esther is also a good cook. Matthew said, "That's great. She and I can make the whole dinner and you can watch us and make sure we're doing it right."

"I'm sure you both will be great, but I will watch." Sandy then called her mom back and told her the good news. Jane said, "I'm so looking forward to it! It has been awhile since we all got together, and now your son will be with us!"

On Saturday, Judy, John, and Esther arrived at their parent's home in the afternoon. They were all so happy to be with each other again. After an early supper, they went over to Sandy and Len's. They wanted to go when Len was there also, and they couldn't wait to meet Matthew.

Sandy introduced Matthew to his aunt Judy, his uncle John and his cousin Esther. They all hugged each other and were so happy. They all sat down and talked.

Matthew and Esther sat aside of each other. Matthew said, "I love your name that comes from the Bible."

"I love your name that comes from the Bible too!" said Esther. They hugged each other.

"You're a wonderful cousin and I'm so glad I met you. I wish we lived closer to each other."

Esther said, "Me too, I'm sure we can get along greatly. I can feel it."

They stayed and talked awhile. Finally, Sandy said to them, "You're going to be shocked when I tell you this, but I'm pregnant!"

"You are! That's so wonderful, but I thought you told me that you wouldn't be able to get pregnant?" asked Judy.

"Len had told me that I can't get pregnant, but he didn't tell me that there was a very slight chance I could. I was shocked when I felt sick and it turned out that I was pregnant. We are so very thankful to the Lord that it did happen. We can't wait! I wonder if it will be a boy or a girl? I'm due around the middle of June and I'm now feeling fine."

Judy, John and Esther hugged them all again and said, "Congratulations! Praise be to the Lord!"

Esther said to Matthew, "Your so lucky that your going to have a brother or a sister. I wish I did. I don't say anything to my parents about it, but now I will have another cousin. I'm looking forward to it."

Judy said, "We'll see you all tomorrow morning. I can't wait to have a meal made by Matthew and Esther. I'm sure it will be great!" They all hugged and kissed each other and they went back to her parent's home.

When they got there, Josh said, "We're so glad you came down to be with us. We wish we could be with you more often."

Judy said, "Me too! I'm sorry that we live so far away in northern Georgia."

"We definitely miss out grandaughter, Esther. She is such a sweet girl. We missed a lot of her growing up," replied Jane.

"Well, let's go to bed. It's getting late and we have to get up early."

The next morning, they all drove to the 8:15 service and sat with Len, Sandy and Matthew. Thelma, Tom, Caleb and Mary Ruth were also there.

After church, they all got together and talked. Caleb said, "Esther, it is so good to see you again. You're starting to be a big girl."

"Yes, we're so glad to see you all again," replied Mary Ruth.

Esther said, "Of course I'm listening to your wonderful Bible study every day and learning so much."

Pastor Ben, Thelma's brother, and his wife, Gloria, came over to them. Thelma introduced them to Judy, John, Esther, and Sandy's son, Matthew. They all shook hands.

Ben said, "We're so glad to meet you all. I just retired from my ministry and we came over to this church today to be with my sister and her family. I'm so glad we did and also got to meet you all. I hope we can see you all again sometime. We're going to Thelma's for dinner."

"One of these days we'll all get together. That would really be fun," said Sandy.

Sandy and her family all went back to her home. Sandy said, "Sorry we had to put some of the kitchen chairs in the living room so you all will have a seat. When dinner is ready, we have to take the chairs back to the kitchen. Thank goodness we have a good sized kitchen and a big table."

Matthew and Esther started making dinner. They made three different vegetables, mashed potatoes, and wonderful roast beef. For desert they were having ice cream with chocolate, caramel, or peanuts on it. As they finally ate, they all loved everything and told Matthew and Esther what great cooks they are.

After they finished eating, they were so full, but happy. Sandy said, "Since Matthew and Esther made such a wonderful meal, it's their turn to sit down and talk to their family. Len and I will do the dishes.

Len said, "Yes, we will be glad to, after that great meal!" They all went back to the living room carrying chairs.

Sandy said, "I'm so sorry about this."

"Don't feel bad, this is about the same size as my house. Remember, you stayed there over ten years ago. We still live in the same house. It's all we need," replied Judy.

Sandy said, "Yes, I surely do remember, but I would love a bigger house since I'm pregnant and will soon have two children. We're kind of filled up now because we brought a lot of Matthew's things down from Georgia. It's even kind of hard for him to get to them, since alot of them are in the garage."

When Len and Sandy finished cleaning up, they went back in the living room and talked. They had a good conversation for a little while.

Judy said, "I'm sorry, but we have to go. It takes awhile to get back to Blairsville, Georgia." They all hugged each other and said "Goodbye, we were so very glad to be with you again." Matthew had told Esther that he wished she lived here.

As they were driving home, John asked, "Esther, are you crying?" Judy looked back at her. She said, "Honey, what's wrong?"

Esther cried louder and said, "I wish we lived in St. Cloud, Florida! I love being with my grandparents, my Aunt Sandy, Uncle Len, and especially my cousin, Matthew! He is so nice and so smart. He told me how his adopted dad was a paster in a Baptist Church in Atlanta. He already understands some of the Bible. He told me that he is praying to the Lord that someday he can work with Caleb, Mary Ruth, and their group. I told him how wonderful that would be, and that I do listen to Caleb and Mary Ruth on the radio, but I would love to learn more and be near them."

"Esther, you know that we always lived in Georgia and we have a good life there."

"I'm sure we would have a good life in St. Cloud with our family, and that was a wonderful church we went to."

Judy said, "Your right, it was very nice being there and the church we went to was great."

They stopped talking and Esther fell asleep. They got home around midnight. John carried Esther out of the car and put her in bed, then went back to his bedroom. Judy was already in bed. She asked John, "Would you even consider on moving down to St. Cloud?"

"Why do you ask me? Do you want to?"

"Maybe Esther is right. It is a nice place and its great being near my family."

"We would have to sell our house, but would we be able to get jobs down there?"

"I really don't know exactly where I can get a job, but I'm sure you can since you're an attorney. Let's just think about it."

"I wouldn't mind moving there if that's what you and Esther want to do. My parents are no longer here. They have both passed away. We will think about it."

Chapter 12

Finally the weekend came when Len, Sandy, Matthew, and Paul went to Georgia. Sandy had called the man who wanted to buy the house and told him when they would be there and that they would be glad to show him the inside.

They got there at 2PM and went into the house. They all walked around and looked. Sandy said, "Wow, this furniture is so pretty. They have a lot of beautiful things here."

She asked Matthew, "What do you want to do with all this furniture and all the things in the kitchen and the garage? There's so much."

Paul said, "If you want, we can come back here again and have a big garage sale, or you can give everything to people who need it."

"I would like to give it all to someone," stated Matthew.

"Well, show us what you want to take back to St. Cloud and we'll start putting it in the truck, after the man looks at the house," said Len.

"Well, the number one things I want are in the family room." They all went to the family room and Matthew showed them all the books on the shelves. He said, "They are all of my adopted dad's many Bible's, study books, and all kinds of Christian books."

Paul said, "Oh boy! That's really great to have all these wonderful books!"

"We're sure going to take them, but we'll have to put everything in the garage and keep the cars outside," replied Len.

Matthew said, "I'm so sorry about filling up the garage."

"Don't worry. We love you." said Sandy.

They walked around and Matthew saw many more things of his that he wanted to take back. A half hour later, they heard the door bell ring.

Sandy went to the door and it was Luke Harney, the man who wants to buy the house. Matthew showed him around, he really loved it.

"I know I want to buy this house!" he said. He asked them how much it was.

Sandy said, "We haven't even thought about it yet. I guess we'll have to check on what the other houses around here are selling for."

"Well, how about I offer you an amount and if it's good, I will go to the bank and find out if they will lend me the money," said Luke. He got a piece of paper out, placed an offer, signed it, and wrote his phone number down. He handed it to Sandy and said, "Give me a call if you like this amount. Bye, hope to see you all again."

Sandy handed the paper to Matthew and said, "Here, this is your house."

Matthew looked at the paper and said, "This looks like a good price." He showed it to Sandy, Len and Paul.

Len said, "It sure does seem like a good amount! Let's check on some of the houses that are for sale and make sure it is good."

They rode around and when they saw a house that was for sale, they would knock on the door and just ask for the price and quickly explain why they wanted to know. Most of the sellers knew Matthew's adopted parents and wished them luck in selling his house.

After they went to four homes, they knew the price that Luke gave them was great, especially considering that they wouldn't even have to pay a real estate commision. They went out, had supper, went back to the house, and filled the truck with all the things they were going to take back to St. Cloud.

Mathew asked Sandy, "Would you please call Luke and tell him that I accept his offer?"

"Sure, I'll call him right now if your neighbor will let me use their phone."

Matthew said, "I'm sure they will. I'll go over with you and introduce you to them." They went over, his neighbors were so glad to see him again and meet his mother. Sandy called Luke and told him that they accept his offer.

He said, "How wonderful! It might be a few weeks before I will find out if I can borrow the money, but I will call you and let you know. I don't think there will be any problem. I have a great job. Once I find out for sure, you will have to come up and sign all the papers. Then you will receive the money."

"No problem, hope to see you soon. Bye, bye," replied Sandy. They thanked the neighbors for using their phone and went back to the house. She told Len and Paul what happened and they all hugged each other.

"It was really great that this happened so fast! I'm sure there is a reason," said Paul. Matthew thought, I think I know what the reason might be. They all went to bed.

When they got up in the morning, they went out for breakfast. Matthew asked, "Can we please go to my church this morning?"

"Sure, we would love to go there," said Len. When they finished eating, they went to the 9:30 service. It was very nice. Matthew knew the new Pastor.

After the service, the Pastor came up to them and hugged Matthew. He said, "Matthew, it's so great to see you again. How are you doing?"

Matthew introduced everyone to him and quickly told him what was happening. Many other people also came up and hugged Matthew. Sandy could tell that everyone really loved him.

They went back to the house, made sure they had everything that Matthew wanted and locked the door when they left. Len and Paul drove the truck and Sandy and Matthew went in Matthew's car. It was a very nice car and Sandy really liked driving it.

When they got back to St. Cloud, they took most of the things into the garage. It did take up a lot of space and no cars could be put in, because they previously had a bunch of things in there also. They invited Paul to supper, and Len handed him money for the gas in his truck that they used.

Paul said, "I don't need the money. You and Sandy need it more than I do. I have to go home and do a few things. I'll see you both at work tomorrow. It was great being with you, Matthew. He gave them all a hug. They thanked him so much. He then left and went back to his home.

Sandy ordered a pizza and they all sat down in the living room. Len said, "Congradulations Matthew! You're getting a good amount of money for your house. We can open a bank account for you and you can use it when you go to college."

"That's a good idea," replied Sandy.

Matthew smiled at them and said. "I will put some of the money in a bank account, but I believe what Paul said is true. This did happen for a reason, and I believe I know what I should do."

Sandy asked, "What could that be?"

"What I want to do is buy you and Len a bigger house."

Sandy and Len were stunned! "No Matthew, you don't have to do that for us," replied Len.

"I know you both would love a bigger house. Your new baby will need a room when he or she gets older and also, you sure would like a bigger living room and bedrooms. You know it will help me to put more things in my bedroom and then we'll be able to put the cars in the garage."

"Are you sure you want to do that," asked Sandy.

"Of course I'm sure! I wouldn't be saying this if I didn't truly mean it."

Len and Sandy hugged and kissed Matthew, They were so happy and thankful! Sandy asked, "Should we put this house up for sale?"

Len said, "We better wait until everything works out with the selling of Matthew's house."

Matthew said, ""That's right, but we can start looking around for a home we might want to buy. I'll be very glad to look with you."

"We can drive around next weekend and check things out." Sandy said.

"I can't wait! I'm looking forward to it!" replied Matthew.

Sandy then called her mom and dad and told them that they were back with a bunch of things from Matthew's house. She didn't tell them the rest of the story and what might be happening. She would rather it happen first, then tell them the good news, so they wouldn't be disappointed if it didn't work out.

On Monday, Sandy and Len went back to work, and Matthew went to school. When the weekend arrived, Sandy and Matthew drove all around the southern part of St. Cloud. They looked at a few houses that were for sale. Sandy kind of liked one but Matthew said, "No, for some reason I think we can find something better."

The next Friday, Luke, the buyer, called and told Sandy everything was ready to go! He asked her if they could come up, be there on Monday at 2 PM, and that it shouldn't take long at all.

Sandy said, "Don't worry, I know my boss will let me take the day off and Matthew can miss one day of school."

Later, she told Len and Matthew the good news. Matthew asked, "Can we go around again this weekend and see other houses that are for sale?"

"Sure we can. This time we'll look in the area that is in the northern section, although we probably won't find anything we can really afford, as those houses are very near the lake.

Matthew said, "That's where Caleb and Mary Ruth live! I would love to live close to them."

"Well, please don't be upset if we can't buy a house there."

"Don't worry, I know that God will lead us and guide us to the house we should buy."

On Saturday they started looking on all the avenues from the east to the west, from 10th street to the lake. There was a few houses they kind of liked. By the time they reached the area of Caleb and Mary Ruth's grandparents home, Sandy said,"Let's stop for today and we can look a little more tomorrow afternoon."

"Okay, can we stop by and say hello to Caleb, Mary Ruth, and their grandparents?"

"Of course we can." They knocked on the door. Tom answered and said, "Hi, how great to see you here, Sandy. We see Matthew during the week but are really glad to see you again."

"I'm sorry I don't get to visit you much, but I work all week and am only off on the weekends. I have a ton of things to do in my house so I hardly leave it."

Thelma walked up and hugged them both. She said, "Congradulations! We heard that your pregnant, how wonderful!"

Matthew said, "I told them. That was okay wasn't it?"

"Of course. Len and I just didn't get to tell many people yet."

"Come in and sit down, Caleb and Mary Ruth are out on the back porch. I'll go get them," said Tom.

They came in and everyone started talking about things. Sandy and Matthew told them what was happening with the home that was left to Matthew, and how they were looking for a bigger home for themselves.

Mary Ruth said, "Hey, did you see the great home that's for sale about two blocks west of here?"

"That's right. Their older people who do not need such a big house now. Their kids are all grown up and they all moved up north. I know it has been for sale for quite awhile but I guess no one is buying it because of the price," replied Caleb.

"We haven't gone west of here yet," replied Sandy.

"Here is the address, but you sure won't miss it when you go by."

They talked for awhile, then Sandy said, "On our way home we'll drive by house and take a look at it."

Chapter 13

When they left, they drove up to the house that Caleb and Mary Ruth told them about. They both said, "Wow!"

"This is truly beautiful, but I'm sure we can't afford it," said Sandy.

"Let's see if their home . I'm sure we can at least see the inside."

"Okay, why not!"

They knocked on the door and an older woman answered. For some reason, she looked sad. Sandy told her that they would like to see the house if it's okay, but they probably can't afford it. They all introduced themselves to each other and Kit said to them, "Come on in, we'll be glad to show you the inside."

They came in and she introduced them to her husband, Vincent, who also had a sad look on his face. They showed Sandy and Matthew all around. The house was even bigger than they were thinking about. They asked the price. Vincent told them what it was. He also told them that a couple days ago it went off the real estate market, so now if we sell it, we don't have to pay them their commission, which was a big amount. So we can really deduct that from the price I told you." He then told them the new price.

Sandy said, "I'm sure that's a great price, but it's more than we can afford." All of a sudden, Kit started crying. Vincent put his arm around her and tears were also coming down his face.

Matthew cried, "What's wrong? Is there anything we can do for you?"

"The problem is, we had this house for sale for quite awhile and hardly anyone looked at it. Even at the price we gave you, I'm sure it won't sell. We want to leave here so badly, so we can be near our children and grandchildren. One of our granddaughters will be having a baby in a few months and we want to be there. Can you make us an offer?"

Sandy and Matthew looked at each other. Suddenly, Matthew said, "A house is being sold next week that we own in Georgia, but it is about twenty thousand less than the price you told us. That's all we can use to buy another house."

Kit and Vincent looked at each other, and cried, "Sold!" Sandy nearly fainted, and said, "Your kidding!"

Kit said, "It's fine!"

"We're so glad you came here today. We were so unhappy and now we're so happy! Thank you so much! Don't worry about it. Just give me your name and phone number and it won't be long until this is your new home!"

Sandy gave them all the information, they then hugged each other and Sandy said, "Thank you so much. Bye."

Sandy and Matthew got in the car. Sandy was crying with happiness and said, "We have to wait a couple of minutes. I'm in shock! Are you sure you want to do this with all the money your getting from your home?"

Matthew said, "I love you all so much! I certainly want to help you. You all surely helped me! If it wasn't for you, Len, Caleb and Mary Ruth, thanks to the Lord, I'd be dead now. I'm also glad that we will be living near Caleb and Mary Ruth. I'm sure this was meant to be!"

Sandy hugged him and said, "I can't wait to tell Len and my parents! They'll be so happy! They both thanked the Lord for leading them to find this house and being able to buy it.

Len and her parents were surprised and so happy about what happened. They all thanked Matthew for being so generous to them.

"I know the Lord has brought me here and is leading me and guiding me to do His will. I am so very thankful to Him and I have complete faith that I will meet my destiny," said Matthew. They all hugged him and told him that they also agree with what he said.

"It is so wonderful to have faith in the Lord and be able to do His will!

THANK YOU DEAR LORD FOR BEING WITH US, LEADING US, AND GUIDING US. WE ARE SO THANKFUL TO YOU AND TRULY BELIEVE, HAVE FAITH AND TRUST

IN YOU. IN THE NAME OF THE FATHER, THE SON AND THE HOLY SPIRIT, AMEN."

On Monday, early in the morning, Sandy and Matthew headed for Atlanta, Georgia. As they were riding, Matthew said, "I just thought of something."

"What is that," asked Sandy.

"Well, Paul was saying how we could have a garage sale before the house get's sold, but now we can use a lot of the furniture and other things in our big, new house."

Sandy smiled and said, "That is true. I'm sure we can rent a big truck to bring whatever we need to St. Cloud."

"Yes, and all the things that are left, we can give to the poor and needy people."

"That's a great idea. Thank you again for your love and kindness."

They arrived an hour early, so they went in the house and decided what they would need. They then went down to the building where the home would be sold. Luke was already there and shook hands with them.

Sandy told him that they would have to come up and remove the furniture. "No problem, my wife and I can afford to buy a lot of new furniture. I have a great job and make great money" replied Luke.

Matthew said, "Boy, that's swell! What do you do?"

"I work with several channels on television and find great shows to be put on them. Others do help me and it's so exciting."

They went in and signed all the papers. Everything worked out fine and they received a check from the bank for the price they sold the house. They both thanked Luke again, and told him that they would be back ASAP to get their things.

"We won't be moving in for about a month. I have to finish some things in California, plus my wife will be looking for a lot of things we want," said Luke.

"We're also buying a home in St. Cloud, that's where everything we take will be going. Since we're paying cash from the home we sold here, it should happen pretty quickly. Thank you again so much for buying this house."

"Thank you again for selling it to me," replied Luke. They all hugged each other and left. Sandy and Matthew got in their car and started driving back to St. Cloud.

As they were driving for awhile, suddenly, they got a flat tire and went off the road. Sandy and Matthew got out and looked at the tire. Sandy said, "Oh no, I never changed a tire before!"

"I'm sure we'll be able to do it," stated Matthew. They got the flat tire off and were trying to put the new one on. Suddenly, a car pulled over and two men jumped out.

Sandy smiled and said, " Thanks for stopping to help us."

The two men looked at them, smiled and one of them said, "Actually, we haven't come to help you. We're just going to do what our boss told us to do." They both pulled out a knife and started coming toward them.

Sandy and Matthew started running and the men started running after them. As the men just about got to them and were about to stab them, a pichup truck flew off the road and hit both men.

Sandy and Matthew saw them laying on the ground and wondered if they were dead. They looked up and the pickup truck disappeared. Next thing that happened, a sheriff's car drove off the road and two officers jumped out and had their guns out.

They saw the two men laying on the ground and one of them said, "What's going on?" Sandy and Matthew explained how they were fixing the flat tire and the two men drove off the road and tried to kill them. They were trying to run away from them, all of a sudden, a pickup truck flew off the road, ran the men over, and disappeared.

The police looked at the two men and noticed that they were still alive, saw that they both had a knife in their hand, and grabbed them. They could tell they were surely hit by a truck. They then radioed for an ambulance. They also noticed the black car. They radioed the police department and had more officers arrive. The other officer said, "We believe your story, but we need your names and address. You also have to come to our police station and tell this story to our captain."

The ambulance was on the way to pick up the unconscious men. The officers checked the men's pockets for their names and addresses, but the pockets were empty. They then checked inside the car and there was nothing there. An officer said, "Why wouldn't these men have a driver's licience or anything with them?"

The ambulance arrived and took the two men to the hospital and the other officers followed them. The first officers fixed Sandy's tire and told her to follow them to the police station. Sandy and Matthew got in the car and started driving.

Sandy was crying, she was so upset. Matthew cried, "THANK YOU DEAR LORD FOR SAVING OUR LIVES! THANK YOU THAT THEY DIDN'T EVEN GET TO HURT US!"

When they arrived at the police station, they told the story to the captain. He said, ""We will do our best to figure out why this happened to you and your son. We're sure you weren't the ones who hurt those men who were trying to kill you both for some reason. We will also try to find out who was driving the pickup truck that hurt the bad men, but saved you both. If we need anything more from you and your son, we will call you. You may leave now as you live in our state of Florida."

Sandy and Matthew finally left and got home really late. Len heard the car come into the driveway and ran outside. He hugged them both and cried, "Is everything okay? What took you so long? Did you have a problem selling the house? I was getting really nervous!"

As they sat down in the living room, Sandy said, "Everything went well with the selling of the house. No problem at all." She and Matthew told him what happened to them when they were a little past Jacksonville, before St. Augustine.

"Thank you Dear Lord, that Sandy and Matthew are okay!" cried Len.

Matthew cried, "He was truly with us and protecting us! We're so very thankful to Him! I truly give myself to Him and promise to do His will!"

They hugged Matthew and Sandy said, "You surely are a wonderful boy!"

"You sure are! We are so thankful to have you. Tomorrow I'm going to call the Jacksonville police department and find out what they have to say about what happened," replied Len. They all got ready and went to bed.

The next day, Len called the police at Jacksonville, he introduced himself to them and told them that he was an officer in St. Cloud. They told him that they are still trying to find out who the bad men are, as they are still unconscious, and who owned their car. They still haven't found the truck that ran over the two men and kept then from killing Sandy and Matthew. We want to find out who was driving that pick up truck. We will keep searching. They told Len that they would call him when they found out more. Len thanked them.

On Wednesday, Vincent called Sandy and told her where the sale would take place on Friday. Sandy said, "We will surely be there with the money! We are so excited!"

On Friday, everything went well. Sandy, Len, and Matthew now owned their new home. Vincent told them that they would be completely gone by Sunday. The next weekend, they rented a big truck and went up to Atlanta, Georgia. They took a lot of the furniture and other things from the house. Everything that was left, they gave to Goodwill, so poor people would be able to buy it cheaply. They drove back to Florida, to their new home. Lots of their friends, including Caleb and Mary Ruth helped them unpack everything. They also brought over a lot of things from their other home.

Sandy asked Len, "What are we going to do with our small house?"

"Let's put it up for sale and whatever we get for it, we will put the money in a bank account for Matthew," suggested Len.

"That's a great idea!" replied Sandy.

They told Matthew what they planned to do. He said, "Thank you, but if you ever need money, feel free to take it."

The first night they stayed at their new home, they were so very happy. Everything was in place and it was so great. They could even put the three cars in the garage, it was huge!

Chapter 14

Sandy's parents, were so very happy for them. They also loved their new home. One day they were sitting with Len, Sandy, and Matthew, talking with them.

Jane said, "Oh, I meant to tell you that I was talking to Judy. She said that they were thinking about moving down here to St. Cloud, but they have to sell their home first and they have no idea how long it will take."

Matthew said, "That is so great! I have an idea. How about we let them stay in the home we just moved out of. We were going to put it up for sale, but we won't. That way they could come down here sooner."

Josh smiled and said, "What a great idea, but it has to be alright with Sandy and Len."

"No problem! We would love to have them move down here," Sandy replied. "Tomorrow I'll call Judy and suggest this to her."

The next day, Sandy called Judy in the evening. She said, "Mom told us that you and your family were thinking about moving to St. Cloud. We will be so happy if you do. Just think, we'd get to spend a lot more time together than we did in the past years."

"Actually, John and I never thought about it. We are so used to living up here where John's parents were, but now they both passed away. When we left St. Cloud a few weeks ago, Esther was crying on the way home and saying that she would love to move to St. Cloud and be with all her family that lived there. That made me start thinking, I should have thought of that. I asked John what he thought and he said that it would be fine with him, providing we would be able to get jobs."

Sandy said, "I only have a few more months to work until I have my baby and I really don't want to work after I give birth. I can recommend you to Captain Hardy so you take over my job. You're just like me and

I'm sure the captain will like you. Till then, you could probably find some little job. What do you think?"

I think it would be great, but where would John work? You know he is an attorney."

"I'm sure our dad can help him find something since he is still the mayor of St. Cloud and he knows a lot of people."

"That's true, anyway, we have to sell our house first."

I know mom was keeping you up to date about how Matthew came into money from his adopted parent's will. Of course you know about how he bought us the big beautiful home, down by the lake."

"Yes, she definitely keeps me informed about everything. She was so happy and excited where you were moving."

"Well, here's the good news! We were going to sell our house, we just moved out of, and with the money we get from it, we were going to put it in a savings account for Matthew. When mom told us that you were thinking about moving down here, Matthew suggested that we don't put the house up for sale. We should let you, John and Esther move in soon. That way, you'll be here when I have my baby!"

Judy cried, "That would be so wonderful! I'll talk to John and Esther as soon as I hang up. Thank you so much!"

"I'll also talk to dad about finding John a job," replied Sandy.

"Okay, talk to you soon! Bye, bye."

When Judy hung up the phone, she went in the living room and sat down with John and Esther, and told them all the good news. Esther jumped up, ran over, and hugged her mom and dad. "I can't wait; we'll be in Sandy's old home which is very near my grandparent's home."

John said, "I have to let my boss know when I'm leaving at least two weeks ahead of time."

"Me too," said Judy. "We also have to tell Esther's school that she'll be leaving when the time comes."

"I'm really looking forward to moving. I just hope I can get a job or we'll be in trouble. We can take out furniture and everything else with us. We'll put this house up for sale with my friend, Adam, the real estate agent."

"That will be fine. We know that Sandy, Len, and Matthew already moved into their new home, so it is okay whenever we move. I am really looking forward to it. I can't wait."

Sandy then called her mom and dad and told them the wonderful news about Judy, John and Esther moving down soon into their empty home. She told her dad that John would need a job as soon as possible.

Her dad replied, "I have a few ideas about jobs he can get, I'll check into them"

Judy and John told their employers and Esther's school that they would be leaving in the next two weeks. They then finished their jobs, packed the truck, after putting their house up for sale, and headed for St. Cloud.

When they arrived at St. Cloud, they stayed overnight at her parent's home and the next day everyone helped them move into their new home. They were all so glad to now be together. They loved each other so much.

Matthew had told Caleb and Mary Ruth how they loved their new home and had lots of room now. Caleb and Mary Ruth were so happy that he was now living near them. Matthew also told them about his Aunt Judy, Uncle John and cousin, Esther moved down from Georgia into Len and Sandy's other house. He told them that his aunt and uncle would be looking for jobs.

Mary Ruth said, "I don't know where your uncle can work, but I'm pretty sure I know where Judy can get a job. A member of our group, Pepi, is one of the top men at Winn Dixie and I think he could get her a job there."

"Boy, that would be great!" replied Matthew.

When he went home, he told his mother about the job Judy can possibly get. Sandy said, "She can work there until I have to stop, then she can take over my job at the police station. She'll be so happy to hear this!"

Judy's dad, Josh, had made a few phone calls to some of his good friends and found out that the county court house would be hiring two attorneys to serve the people that could not afford lawyers. He called John and told him to go to the Osceola Court House with his résumé, ASAP. The next day John went over to the courthouse.

Sandy got in touch with Pepi, and asked him if they might need somebody to work. He said, "Yes, next week one of our ladies is moving away, so we will need someone."

Sandy told him about her sister, Judy, that she and her family had moved down from Georgia. Pepi said, "Send her over to me on Monday morning. I'm sure it will work out." Sandy thanked him then called Judy.

Judy was so happy to hear that she could get a job next week at a grocery store for now. She said, "I'll call Pepi and tell him I will be there on Monday morning."

Sandy said, "I believe that you, John and Esther are supposed to be down here. We're all so glad."

They put Esther in school, she was in the same room as Matthew. By the next week, they both had jobs. They were so happy that they moved to St. Cloud. Now Esther would go with Matthew when he went to see Caleb and Mary Ruth. She loved being with them and all their wonderful friends.

They all had a great Thanksgiving and Christmas. On Christmas, they all got together at Sandy, Len, and Matthew's home. Judy, John, Esther, Jane and Josh, Thelma, Tom, Caleb, Mary Ruth, and their great friend, Paul. They all loved being together and thanked God for everything, especially His wonderful Son, Jesus Christ, their Lord and Savior.

Matthew said, "I also pray that everyone can realize that Christmas is celebrating the birth of Jesus. It is not just a holiday to have fun and give each other presents. Everyone should celebrate the birth of our Lord, Jesus, as the number one thing to do on Christmas." They all said, "Amen."

Chapter 15

By the middle of May, Sandy was getting so very big in her pregnancy. She decided to give up her job at that point, because she was having a hard time walking, let alone working. Everything went well, she showed her sister, Judy, what to do at her new job. Captain Hardy liked her very much and told Sandy that he was so glad to get someone just like her.

All the employees got together, gave Sandy a big cake, told her how they would miss her, and wished her to have a wonderful baby.

That Saturday afternoon on May 21, Sandy started having pain in her abdomen. The baby wasn't due for over three weeks, but the pain was getting worse and worse. Len was at work and Matthew was with Esther at Caleb's. Sandy called Judy, hoping she was home. When Judy answered the phone, Sandy told her what was happening to her.

Judy said, "I'll be right there." She got there in a couple of minutes, but now Sandy was in worse pain. Judy helped her to the car and took her to the hospital.

The doctor checked her right away. He then came back to Judy and said, "Sandy is in extreme labor. She should be having her baby very soon."

The doctor had given her something to ease the pain, never thinking that Sandy would fall asleep. A little while later, nurses took her into the delivery room and helped her push as the doctor was ready to receive the baby. While this was happening already, Judy called Len at work. The police radioed him and told him what was happening. He flew over to the hospital in his police car.

Len was so excited. He said to Judy, "Now I'll finally find out if I'm having a daughter or a son !" They prayed to God that everything would be fine.

A few minutes later, a nurse came out, smiled, and said, "You now have a beautiful son that weighs six pounds, five ounces." All of a sudden, she heard the doctor call her and she ran back in the delivery room.

Len cried, "I pray nothing happened to Sandy or the baby!"

"Let's sit down," said Judy. They held hands and prayed to the Lord that everything was all right.

Five minutes later, the nurse came back out. Judy and Len jumped up and ran over to her. Len cried, "Are they okay!"

The nurse smiled again and said, "They sure are! Even your new daughter!"

Judy and Len just looked at her. The nurse cried, "Your wife had twins!"

They were so very happy! They hugged each other and cried, "Thank You Dear Lord!"

A little while later, Sandy was put in her room and they ran in to see her. They hugged and kissed her. Len said, "It is so very wonderful that we have twins!"

Sandy said, "What? They had given me some medicine for my pain and suddenly, I guess I become unconscious, and I just woke up. I wasn't awake when I had my baby. Your saying that I had twins!"

"Yes, you did! A boy and a girl!" cried Judy.

"Oh thank You, Dear Lord!" cried Sandy.

The nurse happened to walk in. She smiled and said, "I didn't think that Sandy would be awake already. Would you like us to bring the babies in?"

Len cried, "We sure would! We can't wait to meet them!"

"Okay, we'll be back in a few minutes with them. They both are doing well."

Two nurses returned with the two beautiful babies. The one nurse asked, "What are you naming them?"

"We had no idea that we were having twins, we are so thankful to God that we did! We love and thank Him so much! We only thought of a couple names. I know we should make a decision in the next few days." They all held the babies and kissed them.

The other nurse said, "We will bring the twins back in a while and you can start trying to do your breast feeding."

Sandy said, "I can't wait! I hope it works." The nurses took the babies back to the room where they kept all the babies that had just been born.

"Let us thank the Lord for the wonderful thing he has done for us. They held hands and Sandy prayed,

"THANK YOU DEAR GOD FOR GIVING US TWO BEAUTIFUL CHILDREN. PLEASE BE WITH THEM AND HELP US TAKE GOOD CARE OF THEM FOREVER. WE NEVER THOUGHT WE WOULD HAVE ANY CHILDREN, BUT THANKS TO YOU WE ARE SO HAPPY AND GRATEFUL. THEY WILL BECOME GOOD CHRISTIANS AND WILL LEARN ABOUT AND BELIVE IN YOUR WONDERFUL SON, JESUS CHRIST, OUR LORD AND SAVIOR. THANK YOU AGAIN! AMEN."

Len said, "We have to call your parents and Matthew, who is at Caleb and Mary Ruth's home. In fact, I will drive down, get him, and bring him here to see his new brother and sister!" Len went and jumped in his police car to get Matthew.

Judy called their mom and dad and told them the wonderful news. They were so excited! Jane said, "We'll be right over! We can't wait to see out new grandchildren!"

Len knocked on Caleb and Mary Ruth's door. Mary Ruth opened it and said, "Hi Len"

He hugged her and said, "I have to tell you all some great news."

Mary Ruth said, "My grandparents are in the living room and I'll run out and get Caleb and Matthew."

When they all got together, Len cried, "Sandy gave birth today!" They all jumped up, hugged and kissed him.

Then Len cried out again, "She not only had one baby, but she had two, a boy and a girl!"

Matthew yelled, "Thank the Lord! Now I have a brother and a sister!" They were all so amazed and so happy.

Caleb said, "Lets say a prayer for those two children. They all closed their eyes and Caleb prayed,

"THANK YOU EVER SO MUCH FOR GIVING SANDY AND LEN TWO MORE CHILDREN, THAT WAS SO WONDERFUL OF YOU. WE PRAY THAT THEY WILL LEAD A GREAT, HEALTHY, LOVING LIFE. WE KNOW THAT THEY

WILL ALSO BECOME GOOD CHRISTAINS AND BELIEVE IN OUR SAVIOR, JESUS CHRIST. WE WILL TEACH THEM AS YOUNG CHILDREN ABOUT THE BIBLE. THEY WILL TRULY HAVE A LOVING LIFE AND WILL KNOW HOW TO FOLLOW YOUR WILL AND WALK IN YOUR PATH OF RIGHTEOUSNESS AND HOPEFULLY, WILL NEVER LEAVE IT. WE THANK YOU AGAIN. IN JESUS NAME, AMEN."

They all hugged each other again. Len said, "Come on Matthew, I'll take you to the hospital to meet you new brother and sister and see how well you mother is doing."

Thelma said, "Tell Sandy how happy we all are for your family. Tom, Caleb, Mary Ruth and I will come to see her and the new babies tomorrow after church."

"That will be great, Sandy is so happy and our babies are so beautiful! We want to name them before she leaves the hospital, so we have to start thinking. See you all tomorrow."

They went back to the hospital. Matthew ran over, hugged and kissed his mom and said, "I am so excited to see the babies!"

Len said, "Come on, I'll take you to look at them through the window." Len showed Matthew his new brother and sister.

"They are really beautiful! I am so very happy and thankful to the Lord!"

"So are we! You can help us think what we should name them. We aren't going to name them after us, but good people in the Bible, as your name is." Sandy's mom and dad were there now and they couldn't wait to hold their new grand children.

Judy said, "I'm going to run home and bring John and Esther over, if it's okay."

"Of course it is!"

"I'll be back soon."

Len, Sandy, Matthew and her parents started thinking about names for the babies. They thought about boy's names first, and decited to name their son David. Sandy said, "I think a great middle name would be Joshua, plus it is my dad's name. They all shook their heads up and down. Sandy's dad hugged everyone and said, "Thank you, I'm so glad I have a name from the Bible. David and Joshua are from the Old Testament and are both very Godly men."

They were then trying to think of a great woman's name. Matthew said, "How about Elizabeth, the mother of John the Baptist? She is in the New Testament"

"I think that would be wonderful," replied Sandy.

"Me too! Thank you so much Matthew! How about we name her Elizabeth Ruth? Does that sound good?" They smiled and shook their heads up and down.

"We now have David Joshua and Elizabeth Ruth as our children!" said Sandy.

They were all so happy and thankful for the twins. Sandy and Len were great parents and Matthew was a great big brother. Sandy's parents helped them all the time. The babies were growing up healthy and strong. They all loved them so much and the babies loved their family.

Chapter 16

When the babies were four years old, David and Elizabeth were in great shape. Every Sunday, they went to the children's Bible study at church and Matthew also taught them about the Bible and their Lord Jesus Christ. It was now the early eighties.

Caleb was now twenty-six years old and Mary Ruth was twenty-three. In the last few years, Caleb and Tammy totally fell in love with each other. They planned to get married on June 21st at the Baptist Church. Mary Ruth and Mike were also in love. Mary Ruth was going to be Tammy's maid of honor and two of her good friends were going to be the bridemaids. Mike, Pepi and Raymend would be Caleb's grooms. Matther and Esther were now sixteen and they would seat the people. They decidied to have little David and Elizabeth walk up the isle first and throw little flowers around.

They were all still doing their teachings on the radio at 6AM. The day of the wedding finally arrived. After the others went down the aisle before them, Tammy's father walked with her down the aisle to marry Caleb. Everyone was so happy and many people attended the wedding. There were also some people from the news that were there and took a little film of Caleb, Tammy, and their wedding group. The wedding and reception was wonderful. The next day, Caleb and Tammy went on a honeymoon to Israel and went on an excursion to see many things. They loved it so much, seeing where Jesus was.

Caleb said to Tammy, "This is the most wonderful honeymoon we could have ever had!" They were both so happy.

Tammy said, "We can now tell the people that are listening to our teachings on the radio about all the things we have seen here. I'm sure they will really like it."

"I believe a lot of the people would love to hear about it. To bad we couldn't show them some pictures or the video we're talking."

After the wedding, the world news on television, showed Caleb and Tammy's marriage and of course told everyone that they had Bible teachings on the radio for several years.

It so happened that Luke Hardy and his wife, Elaine (the couple that bought Matthew's home in Georiga)were watching the news and seen Caleb, Tammy, and their wedding group. Luke said, "We know them! Their teachings are so wonderful!"

Elaine said, "They sure are! I am so glad our kids listen to them everyday before they leave for school."

"I just got a thought in my head! Beside Caleb, Tammy and Mary Ruth they have a great group teaching with them. I am thinking, that they could have a great television show on Sundays if I can make arrangements for it."

"Oh boy, that would really be nice! I know a lot of people who listen to their teachings, Monday through Friday. I'm sure they would love to see them on television."

"First of all, I'll find out if they are interested in doing a TV show, if they are, I'll try to find them a spot. I hope they will be able to pay for it, but usually, if people love the Christian show, they will donate money to them so they can keep on. I'm sure Matthew is at least sixteen years old by now. I'll talk to him and his mother about this and see what they think."

That evening, Luke called Sandy and Matthew. He introduced himself to Sandy and she remembered him. He told her how he saw Caleb and Tammy's picture from their wedding on the news and suddenly the thought of them having a TV show entered his mind.

Sandy told him that Caleb and Tammy were still on their honeymoon in Isreal, but she and Matthew will be glad to tell Mary Ruth and the others about the great thought you have.

"Okay, let me know what they think about this and I will try my best to get them a place on Sunday's. They also will be taught how to do a television show and the exact time they have to do everything."

"Thank you so much! Caleb will call you soon and let you know. Bye, bye."

When Sandy hung up the phone, she ran into the living room

where Len, Matthew, David, and Elizabeth were playing games. She said, "Listen everybody, you will be so excited when you hear what just happened!" She then told them what Luke Hardy said on the phone.

Matthew said, "I do remember when we sold the house to him that he said he had a great job. How wonderful that he thought of this! I believe that the Lord told his mind to do this! I hope it all works out!"

"How wonderful! Caleb, Mary Ruth and their group will be so excited!" said Len.

"How about Matthew and I run over now to Caleb's home? I know Caleb isn't there, but we can tell Mary Ruth."

"Okay, I'll stay here and play with David and Elizabeth. See you soon."

Sandy and Matthew ran over to see Mary Ruth and knocked on the door. Tom opened the door and said, "Hi, what a surprise to see you at this time."

"That's because we really have a surprise to tell you all. Is Mary Ruth here?"

"Oh yes, her, Mike, Pepi and Raymond are in the family room working on their teachings."

"Can we please interupt them? It's important."

"Of course, can Thelma and I also hear the news?"

"Of course! Lets all go in the family room," said Sandy. Thelma came over and they all went into the room.

Mary Ruth and the group all looked up and saw Sandy and Matthew. They all jumped up and hugged them. Mary Ruth said, "Hi, it's so nice to see you both.!"

Matthew said, "You'll think it is really nice when we tell you why we're here!"

"Please tell us, we can't wait to hear," replied Mike.

"Mom, tell them the great news!"

"I got a phone call from Luke Harney, the man who bought Matthew's adopted parents home. He mentioned that he saw Caleb and Tammy's marriage on the news and suddenly, he got a thought in his mind."

Pepi asked, "What could that be?"

"Well, believe it or not, he has a great job putting great shows on TV. He thought how wonderful it would be for you all to have an hour show on Sundays!" Mary Ruth and the three men jumped up and hugged each other.

Mike said, "That would be so wonderful if we could do that!"

"I'm in shock, what wonderful news!" cried Raymond.

"Tammy and Caleb will be back in a few days. What a wonderful wedding present this is!" said Mary Ruth.

Thelma and Tom thanked them very much and said, "What wonderful news!"

"As soon as you tell Caleb and Tammy and talk with them, call me and tell me your decision. Also, I want you to know that it will probably cost you some money to do this, but I don't have any idea how much."

Thelma said, "We will figure something out to pay for it."

"Of course we will," said Tom.

They all jumped up and down and hugged each other again. "We can't wait to tell this to Caleb and Tammy when they get back!"

"Okay, I have to go home to put my sweet little twins to bed," said Sandy.

Matthew said, "We'll be waiting to hear from you." They went back home and Sandy told Len how excited everyone was and will call as soon as they talk to Caleb and Tammy when they get back."

"Okay kids, time for bed, let's get going." The two kids jumped up. They went to the bathroom, brushed their teeth, put their pajamas on, said their prayers, and jumped in their twin beds. Len, Sandy, and Matthew kissed them goodnight.

"I'm also going to bed. I have some Bible reading to do. The more I read, the more I understand. Goodnignt, I love you both," said Matthew.

Len said, "We might as well go to bed and read the Bible. It doesn't matter how many times we read it, or how old we are, you always do understand more and more."

"I know we can understand a lot when we read it together. I thank God that we have such a great life. We truly love and have faith in Him."

"He always helps us, when it is due, no matter what happens. Thank You, Dear Lord!"

The next day, when they got up and went downstairs, David and Elizabeth had a children's show on TV. A song was playing and the kids were singing. Len said, "Wow Sandy, I had no idea that the kids had such great voices. That's really neat!"

While Sandy was making breakfast, Matthew came in the kitchen. "Good morning Mom!" They hugged each other.

"Guess what? Len and I heard David and Elizabeth singing a song this morning. They sounded so good!"

Matthew said, "I heard them singing many times. They sure do have great voices as little kids."

"Their really great!" said Sandy. Breakfast was ready, Sandy, Matthew, and the kids ate. Len had already gone to work.

Several days later, Caleb and Tammy came home from their honeymoon. For now, Tammy was staying with Caleb at his grandparents home, since they did all their planning there with the others. Thelma and Tom loved Tammy so much and she loved them also.

They all sat down together in the living room. Caleb said, "We had such a wonderful time! It was amazing!"

"It was so fastastic being in Isreal, seeing where Jesus was, where he preached to people and had done so many miracles. We love our Lord so much! If any of you can ever go there, you will be totally amazed! I am so glad we went there! It made us both even happier," said Tammy.

Caleb and Tammy told them what they did every day in Jerusalem and the other places. They were all so happy about what they heard.

Tammy asked, "Has anything happened while we were gone?"

"You both will be so very happy when you hear what happened!" cried Mary Ruth.

"What happened?" asked Caleb.

Mary Ruth told them how Sandy and Matthew came over a few nights ago and what they heard from a man named Luke Harney, the man who bought Matthew's house in Georgia. She explained what he told Sandy about our group having a show on TV, every Sunday for an hour!"

Caleb and Tammy looked at each other and said, "Thank you so much Dear Lord!"

"I'm sure he wanted this to happen for us. He always leads us and guides us to do His will. We did say many prayers in Jerusalem and thanked the Lord for all He has done for us all our lives. We also prayed that we would completely meet our destiny. Being on television should have us bring more and more people to Him." replied Caleb.

"We will have to learn how to do the show, they said that Luke would have someone give us many ideas as to what we can do. We also have to pray that we'll be able to pay for the TV show," said Mary Ruth.

Thelma said, "We definitely will help you."

Tammy smiled and said, "I can't wait to tell my parents and grandparents what is happening! I'm sure they will also help us."

"Let's call Sandy and tell her how we feel about it!"

Caleb called her and told her that they definitely want to try it, pray that it does good, and it keeps doing good.

Sandy said, "I was hoping that you and Tammy would also feel this way. I'll call Luke and tell him the good news."

Caleb asked, "Can I please say hello to Matthew?"

"You sure can." She called Matthew to the phone.

Matthew said, "Isn't this news wonderful!"

"It sure is! This has happened because of God and your home in Georgia. If you weren't here, this might not have happened. Thank you for your help! We'll get together with you and Esther and tell you all about our honeymoon in Israel. It was awesome! See you tomorrow."

"I'm so thankful that you had a great time in Israel and also so glad you will have a television show. Bye, bye."

Chapter 17

Sandy called Luke and told him that Caleb, Mary Ruth and their group truly would love having a TV show. They are so grateful to you for offering it to them. Here is their phone number so you can call and tell them exactly how they have to understand how to do everything on television."

"Thank you so much for helping me. I'll give them a call right now!"

Luke called and Caleb answered the phone. "Hi, my name is Luke Harney, I'm so glad you are willing to do a TV show. I have listened to you and your group teachings on the radio for years. I thought I knew the Bible until I started listening to your teaching. I have learned so much and now understand many more things the Bible says. I'm sure you all can help many more people become Christians in this whole country by having them see you all on television and realizing why they should believe in Jesus Christ, our Lord and Savior, and what He has done for us. Everyone should thank, love, and have faith in Him. The more Christians there are in this country, the better this country will be and can truly help other countries."

"You are totally right, we want to keep our destiny with God. We love the Lord so very much!" replied Caleb.

"Maybe someday we can get together. That would be great. Meanwhile, I have to find out exactly what channel I can put your show on and what time. If it's okay with you, I will send a couple of my members down to you in St. Cloud, to explain good ways to do your shows. That way your whole group won't have to come up to Georgia."

"That will be great! When will they come?"

"How about as soon as I find where and when I can place you. Then they will come down and talk with you all. It shouldn't be too long from now." Caleb gave him their address.

Luke said, "I will get in touch with you soon. By the way, what started this was, I saw a picture of you and your wife on the news and heard that you lived in St. Cloud. I knew that was where Matthew was now living with his real mother. I called them and was so glad that they were good friends with you and your group. By the way, you have a beautiful new wife!"

"Thank you, I love her so much and I know that the Lord has brought her to me. She is a very great, smart, loving Christian, and of course, part of our teaching group. We'll all be looking forward to hearing from you and I'm sure your people that are coming will really help us to have good shows. The main thing is, we always want to do things about the Father, Son and Holy Spirit."

"I'll be calling you soon, Caleb! Take care. Bye, bye." Caleb hung up the phone and told Tammy, Mary Ruth and his grandparents what was going to start happening. They were all so excited.

Mary Ruth said, "I can't wait to tell Mike, Pepi, Raymond and all our others about this. We'll see them all tomorrow."

When they all got together the next day, they were all so thrilled about the TV shows. They all prayed and thanked God so much for His love and having them do His will. They also prayed that they can have people understand about Jesus Christ, ask for forgiveness of their sins, and become good loving Christian people.

Three days later, Caleb received a call from Luke. He said, "I have great news for you! I can get you an hour show at 7 PM on Sunday evening on a good channel. What do you think about that time?"

"I think it will be fine! Usually people are finished eating supper by then."

"Your first show will take place a month from now on September 28. Therefore, you have a good amount of time to decide what you are going to do. Remember, we have commercials on that channel. When my people come down to help you, they can take some pictures and a little video of you all to advertise your new show. A lot of people in Florida and Georgia know you, but not the people in the rest of the country. Hopefully, a lot more people will start watching your new show. Make your first show really good. If it is, they will probably keep watching and you will become very famous. If it is okay with you, I will send my people down in three days."

"That will be great! We can't wait to learn and understand how to do everything."

"Okay, they have your address and will be there as soon as they get to St. Cloud. They'll probably stay there for at least a week as we know you still do your Bible studies on the radio every morning."

"Thank you so much, Luke. We will do our best. We are so excited! Bye."

Three days later, a woman named Lois, and a man named James, came to their home. They introduced themselves to Caleb and Mary Ruth. Mary Ruth introduced them to all their wonderful group. They all sat down. Lois and James explained to them how they should do things during the show in different ways so it would keep people's attention, also do things so they wouldn't be bored.

Lois said, "What you all are going to do will be wonderful, but there will be many people watching who won't understand what your talking about. You have to teach them in many different ways. Don't forget, it won't be only adults watching. There will be young people, old people, teenagers, even little kids. I know you want them all to learn, you can do many different things so everyone will watch."

They went on and on. The group asked many questions and took many notes, so they wouldn't forget anything. After four hours, Jim asked, "Do you have any more questions? I'm sure we told you everything and we wish you the best of luck."

Tammy said, "Let us pray." They all held hands and thanked the Lord for all He has done for them to bring more and more people to Jesus Christ.

"I'm sure your show will be so wonderful. Jim and I will be here for the next week and we can really help you with any of your questions and the way you would like to do things. We're going back to the hotel now and we'll see you tomorrow. It was great being with all of you great young Christians," replied Lois.

When they left, the group started talking about what exactly to do since they now know how much time they have between the commercials. Tammy said, "I know we're going to teach great things but I think it would be great if we could have Matthew and Esther teach teenagers on some of the shows. I know it was really good when we did that at our Bible studies when we were in high school.

"That's a really great idea! I will call and have them come over tomorrow after school. We can ask them if they would like to do that," said Caleb.

The next day, Matthew and Esther came over. Matthew said, "I hope every thing is working out for your new TV show."

Mary Ruth introduced them to Lois and Jim. She told the kids how they were helping them learn how to do the shows.

Caleb said, "My wife, Tammy, came up with a great idea yesterday. She said that in some of the shows it would be wonderful if you and Esther could do some teaching for teenagers."

Esther cried, "You mean we can be on your TV show?"

"We would truly love to do that. Esther and I are like you all. We love the Lord and want to bring more and more people to Him. A lot of teenagers don't go to church because their parents work or do other things. They don't even know who Jesus really is, or the Bible."

"That is so wonderful! We'll be more than glad to do it," replied Esther.

Lois asked, "You mean you teenagers know a lot about Jesus Christ and the Bible?"

"We surely do! He is our everything, I feel that Esther and I will be starting to meet our destiny by doing this," said Matthew.

Jim said, "Sounds wonderful to me!" They all hugged each other and started talking about how they have to rehearse and have everything right for each show.

Matthew said, "I have a suggestion. I hope you like it. Maybe in some of the shows there can be two little kids singing great Christian songs for any children that might be watching with their parents."

"That's a good idea, if the group would like to do that." said Lois.

"That would be great, but where are we going to find little children who are good singers?" asked Mary Ruth.

"Believe it or not, my little sister and brother, David and Elizabeth, are truly great singers. I hear them singing every day while they are watching television. They already know some Christian songs from Sunday School."

"That s a great idea. Do you think they will want to do it?" asked Tammy.

"Sandy and Len, my parents will be so very excited when they heard about us being on your TV show. When my parents hear about their little four year old twins singing on your show, they will be even more excited. I just hope that David and Elizabeth want to do it and do good."

"I'm sure they will," said Caleb. "It's getting late, do you and Esther need a ride home?"

Matthew said, "I now have my drivers license and I'm driving a car that used to belong to my adopted parents. Anyway, Esther's mom, dad and our grandparents are going to be at my house having supper with us."

"We can't wait to tell them the great news. We'll see you tomorrow, bye, bye," said Esther.

They went over to Matthew's home just in time for supper. They all sat down at the table and had a good meal. Esther then said, "We have some wonderful news to tell you when we finish our desert."

Sandy asked, "Can you give us a hint now?"

"No, if we tell you anything now you'll probably never even finish your desert.!"

"Hurry everybody, let's finish, so we can hear the news," said Len. When they finished, they left everything on the kitchen table and ran and sat in the living room. Sandy had the little twins sit with her and Len.

Esther's mom said, "Okay, here we are, tell us the news!" Esther told them how Caleb and his group asked her and Matthew to be on their TV show and teach teenagers. Everybody was so happy and excited!

Sandy said, "How wonderful! I know that Caleb and Mary Ruth have been with you both for quite awhile and truly know how you both would love to help other teenagers like they did years ago when they were in high school. This time you will be helping every teen that watches in the whole country." They all hugged Mathew and Esther and thanked the Lord.

Sandy and Len were going to get up and clean the kitchen. Matthew cried, "Wait a minute! We have something else to tell you!"

Len asked, "What could that be? You already told us the very wonderful thing about you and Esther."

"This is another very wonderful thing!" Esther cried.

Sandy asked. "What else could be that wonderful?"

"Caleb and the group were talking about things to do during the show and I asked, what about the kids who are watching? What might they like to see? Then I told them what great singers David and Elizabeth are. They all said that it would be great to have them on the show and said that every week they can sing a beautiful Christian song and say a few words to children about Jesus if they are willing to do it," Matthew said.

Sandy and Len had happy tears in their eyes. Sandy cried, "Matthew, thank you so much! We will help them learn the songs and how to talk to the kids."

David and Elizabeth didn't really understand what they were talking about. Sandy asked them, "How would you both like to be on a TV show, sing Christian songs, and help children?"

The kids just looked at each other. David asked, "How can we be on TV?"

Elizabeth asked, "Are we really good singers?"

"I know you both are great signers. Others will be so happy to hear you. The TV show will take place at the movie threater in Kissimmee. It will be on Sunday evenings at 7PM. You kids will have to sing what you are told to sing and practice it all week. Do you think you can do it?" asked Matthew.

"I'm sure we can," Elizabeth said. "We want to pray that we will do good." They all prayed and thanked the Lord.

Lisa and James stayed for a few more days and worked with them all. They were so amazed to hear David and Elizabeth sing. James said, "I believe you people are going to have some really great shows. As Luke told you, we will be advertising your show."

Mike said, "I also think we should tell everyone that listens to our Bible studies on the radio about it."

"That sure is a great idea, you are such a wonderful man!" said Mary Ruth.

"Thanks to you all! If it wasn't for you, Caleb, Tammy and Paul, I probably would be in jail for life. I was so nasty! You brought me to the Lord and I am so thankful and grateful to you all."

Caleb said, "That would be a good thing to talk about in one of our shows. You were a nasty person in high school and we did keep trying and trying to bring you to the Lord. It did finally happen years later. You started like Paul in the New Testament, how Jesus brought him to be a wonderful Christian disciple and have many gentiles become Christians."

Lois and Jim hugged them all. Lois said, "We wish you all the best of luck with your shows and we'll be watching them." They went back to Georgia.

Caleb, Mary Ruth and the group worked every day, put shows together and wrote everything down. They worked with Matthew and Esther and gave little David and Elizabeth the songs they wanted them to sing on each show and what they wanted them to say to the children.

A week before the first show, they rehearsed many times and everything seemed to be going fine. Luke sent three men down from Georgia who would come and film the show every week and make sure that they are doing everything right.

Finally, the first Sunday arrived and they all were ready and excited. They also were a little nervous, but they knew that the Lord would be with them. The show started with Caleb and Mary Ruth standing together. They smiled and introduced each other to the people that were watching and told them how grateful they were for this television show. They then introduced all the others. Caleb's wife, Tammy, Mike, Pepi, Raymond, Matthew, Esther, David, and Elisabeth.

The older group all sat down and spoke about Jesus Christ and why everyone should believe in Him and become great Christian people. In a ten minute section, Matthew and Esther talked with teenagers that were watching and tried to help them understand why they should now become Christians. David and Elizabeth sang a song called, "I Come To The Garden Alone." They sounded so wonderful, then said a few words to the young children.

Caleb explained how they would be teaching all about the Lord in every show. The show ended with them all holding hands, praying for everyone in the world, and thanking God for all He has done. They all waved and Caleb and Mary Ruth said, "See you next Sunday!" The show ended and they all hugged each other.

The three man came up to them, smiled, and one of them said, "You all did a great job! I'm sure we'll be coming down here for a long time."

All the people they knew told them how they truly loved the show and couldn't wait to see the next one. They all were so happy to hear the good news.

Two days later, Luke called Caleb's home. Caleb answered the phone and Luke said, "Congradulations! There was a huge number of people watching your show, and I got great comments about it. You all really did a great job!"

"Thank you so much! I pray that we can bring more people to believe in Jesus. We plan to talk about many things in the Bible. The Old and New Testament, so people will be able to learn and understand things they never did understand before."

"I know you will have many more great shows. I will keep in touch with you and let you know what people are saying about it. Take care. I'm so glad I was able to put you and your wonderful group on TV. I also love the name of your show, "Learn, Believe, and Obey." Bye."

Everything went very well for the next few months. On one of the shows they showed their video of Israel when Caleb and Tammy were on their honeymoon. Everyone seemed to love it with the comments they received. Many people were now watching their show and were sending many donations to help them stay on TV. They all were so happy and thankful to the Lord.

Chapter 18

Christmas came and everyone really loved their show. They all sang great songs and explained how celebrating the birth of Jesus is number one on Christmas day. It's okay to give presents and have Christmas trees, but always be thankful for Jesus Christ first, pray to Him, and thank Him for what He did for us by dying on the cross so our sins would be forgiven and we can come to His Father, God, through Him.

On Christmas day, they all got together in the afternoon at Caleb and Mary Ruth's home to be thankful for the birth of Jesus on the day it was being celebrated, although it was not the real day He was born.

Sandy, Len, Matthew, Elizabeth, David, Judy, John, Esther, Jane, Josh, Ben, Gloria, Thelma, Tom, Paul, and of course, Tammy, Mike, Pepi, and Raymond were all with Caleb and Mary Ruth. They all loved each other so much and were having sweet conversations.

All at once, Mike stated loudly, "I would like to have your attention please." Everyone stopped talking and looked at him. Mary Ruth was standing at his side.

Mike said, "I am so thankful to God that I have become closer and closer to Him, and am now doing His will. I love Him so and thank Him with all my heart, soul, and mind, that I now walk in His path of righteousness. Thanks to Caleb, Tammy and Paul for saving me that day. Now I want to do something that will also be wonderful for me." He looked at Mary Ruth, got down on his knees, and said, "Mary Ruth, I love you so much and thank the Lord for you, I pray that you feel the same way." He reached in his pocket, got a ring, and placed it on her finger. "Mary Ruth, will you please marry me? I promise to be a wonderful husband, love you, and care for you forever."

Tears were running down Mary Ruth's eyes. She cried, "I thank

God for you, I'm sure He will be with us and give us a great life. Of course I'll marry you!"

Mike jumped up and they hugged and kissed. Everyone clapped, ran over and hugged and kissed both of them. Caleb said, "I pray you will have a great life together like Tammy and I do. We love you both so much!" They were all so happy and thanked God for the wonderful day.

Everything was going really fine. During the second show in January, while it was on TV, a strange man ran up on the stage in front of them. He screamed, "Don't believe a word you hear from these people. None of it is true!" He then ran off the stage and disappeared.

Caleb jumped up and said, "We have no idea who that man was, and why he said what he did. Please do not listen to him. Believe in God and His son Jesus Christ always." When the show ended they were all upset over what the man did.

Caleb said, "I know our show is doing great and I believe more people are becoming Christians. I pray that Satan has not come to take people away from the Lord! I pray that will never happen again."

The next few weeks went by and it didn't happen. The shows were great but they found out that a lot of people had stopped watching it.

Tammy asked, "What could be causing this to be happening? Just because that one crazy man ran up on the stage during the show and screamed those crazy words? Why would people listen to him?"

"Somehow, someway, I have a feeling that something else is happening," replied Mary Ruth.

A thought came into Caleb's mind to talk to some of his friends. Later he went over to one of his high school friend's house, named Nick. He knocked on the door and Nick opened it and said, "Hi Caleb, come on in." They went into the living room and he introduced Caleb to his new wife, Marie. They shook hands and sat down.

Nick said, "We still watch your Sunday show on television. We love it and all your wonderful people who are amazing. We truly love all the teachings and those two little twin singers are so great!"

"Thank you so much. Did you know that Mary Ruth and Mike got engaged on Christmas?"

"How wonderful!" said Nick.

"The main reason I came over tonight is to ask you a question. For some reason, a lot of people have stopped watching our TV show. Do you have any idea what might be causing this?"

"Don't worry, we will never stop watching your TV show and listening to the radio teachings. They are so great and we will never stop beliving in the Lord 100%! I do have an idea of what might be happening. We watch TV up to 11PM at night, then we go to bed. When the commercials come on, I just usually click over to other channels and see what's going on. A couple weeks ago, I clicked on a show on channel 66. I was going to click off again, when I heard a man mention the name of Caleb and Mary Ruth. I stayed there and they were talking about your TV show and your radio Bible teachings. They were saying how wrong everything was and that everyone should stay away from the teachings. I guess they also said other things about you and Mary Ruth and the people who were watching them started beliving what they said, and probably told others. They did that more than once on their show."

Caleb said, "I'm sure that is probably what happened. Those men are unbelievers in Jesus and probably have evil spirits in them from Satan. Jesus Christ is truly the Son of God and our Lord and Savior. We're going to have to be more progressive in all our studies. We need to bring the people back."

Nick said, "We will never leave our Lord, no matter what anyone says."

"That is wonderful, I wish all people were true believers. I really appreciate you telling me this. Now I know what is happening. Satan is here again, trying to stop us from meeting our destiny, which is to bring people to Jesus Christ and God His Father. Thank you so much for your help. See you at church, and it was great to meet your new wife. Take care, bye."

The next day Caleb told Mary Ruth, Tammy, Mike, Pepi and Raymond what Nick told him was on some TV show. Mary Ruth said, "Let us not worry! We will beat Satan!"

Suddenly, they heard some very loud thunders in the sky and a loud voice say,

"NOT THIS TIME! I WILL MAKE THE PEOPLE BELIEVE ME AND BE AGAINST YOU ALL!"